TIME SENSITIVE

A Time Travel Novel

Elyse Douglas

Broadback Books

Copyright © 2019 Elyse Douglas

All rights reserved

The characters and events portrayed in this book are fictitious. Any similarity to real persons, living or dead, is coincidental and not intended by the author.

No part of this book may be reproduced, or stored in a retrieval system, or transmitted in any form or by any means, electronic, mechanical, photocopying, recording, or otherwise, without express written permission of the publisher.

ISBN-13: 9798481942001

Cover design by: Art Painter
Library of Congress Control Number: 2018675309
Printed in the United States of America

For Lillian: Thanks for the newspaper article.

"Time flies over us but leaves its shadow behind."
--Nathaniel Hawthorne

TIME SENSITIVE

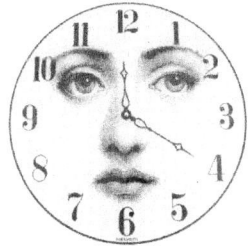

PART 1

CHAPTER 1

In 1968, when I was twenty-six years old, my husband and two daughters perished in a fire. Paul, Lacey, and Lyn all died—gone in a flash, in a senseless accident—gone from my life forever.

Until recently, I had taken pride in the belief that I had moved on with my life. After all, the tragedy had occurred many years before and people are expected to push away the memories and let time heal all things. People are expected to recover and find the strength and the will to keep going on with their lives. And that's exactly what I had done, or thought I had done, until lately.

It was after I retired and was diagnosed with atherosclerosis that the old ghosts began to awaken and lift their heads, especially deep in the night. They brought back the darkness, the guilt and the regret. As I lay in bed, I could smell the spring scent of the girls as they slept. I could see Paul lingering in a shadowy corner, his expression tender, his fingers beckoning. My sick heart began to ache, just as it had all those years ago.

I knew I should have bypass surgery, but I kept putting it off. I don't know why. I'm usually aggressive and a good problem-solver. I'm not a procrastinator, but as the days progressed, I awoke to the disheartening realization that my heart had never truly mended. It was still broken, as shattered as it was on Wednesday, June 5, 1968. What truly hurts, and has been broken, cannot be cured by bypass surgery.

In 1968, I was one of the few women who worked for the NSA in Fort Meade, Maryland. I was the only female linguist analyst; I had always been proficient in languages and spoke French, German and Spanish fluently. While NSA stands for the National Security Agency, we often called it "No Such Agency," because we were a secret agency, responsible for tracking Communists, peace activists, black and white radicals, civil rights leaders, and even drug peddlers. My job, specifically, was focused on crypto systems and intelligence interpretation. As the volumes of data came flooding in, I extrapolated and distilled it into clear, concise and potentially useful facts. It wasn't easy, and it took hours and weeks and months to sort through the often trivial and useless mountains of files and codes to find only a word or a sentence or a series of numbers that were worthy of being quarantined or flagged as possibly urgent and valuable.

I was good at it—not my words, but my boss's

words, Steven Case's words. There were no personal computers in 1968, and although we had some impressive technology for our day, it couldn't compare with the technological capabilities of today. In those days, intelligence gathering was tedious, time-consuming, mind-numbing and impressionistic, at best. An IBM Mainframe, with its 256k memory and punch cards, did some analysis, and we human analysts did the rest.

I worked too many hours, worked too many weekends and ignored my family, and, in the end, I paid dearly for it. Of course, after the tragedy occurred, I saw things more clearly—don't we always in hindsight? Doesn't the fog lift and the full flood of baking sun reveal all our failings and bad choices—all our painful regrets?

I had arrogantly taken my family for granted and when they were snatched away from me in that sudden, awful and violent way, I saw how utterly selfish and stupid I'd been. But it was too late. As they say, what's done is done. You can't go back—at least I couldn't go back then—to 1968.

But then there was my friend, Luke, who suggested the impossible, that perhaps I *could* go back in time and right all the wrongs. Assuming, of course, that I wasn't killed in the process.

CHAPTER 2

I first heard about Cyrano Conklin and TEMPUS from Luke Baker, a former colleague at the National Security Agency. Luke and I had worked together for many years and we had retired around the same time. Luke was also one of the few people still alive who knew about my personal tragedy, although we hadn't discussed it in years.

Luke called me one Saturday morning in February 2018 and invited me to breakfast. We met at the Pancake House and I ordered eggs, bacon, white toast and coffee. Luke got the blueberry pancakes. After we had ordered, he asked me an intriguing question.

"Can you keep a secret?"

"Is that a joke? I've kept secrets my entire life, Luke. So did you. That's what we did for a living."

"This is a big secret. As they used to say, this is one of the mother-of-all-time secrets."

I kept waiting for his explanation and he kept putting me off, saying he needed the fortification of pancakes before he could talk business.

Finally, he pushed his empty plate aside and leaned back. "I hope you're not angry at me, Charlotte, but I did something quite on impulse."

"That's not like you," I said. "When was the last time either of us did anything on impulse? We're not the impulsive types."

"Exactly," Luke said. "But we're not getting any younger, are we? I'll be seventy-seven years old in two weeks. You just turned seventy-six, right?"

"Yes," I said, searching his eyes, wondering what he was up to.

Luke had white hair, a bit of a paunch, and steady blue eyes. He wore Benjamin Franklin style wire-rimmed glasses that made him look a bit owlish and very intellectual.

"So what have you done, Luke?" I asked, pushing my plate away and sipping coffee. "The eggs and pancakes are gone. Out with it."

He leaned in and spoke at a near whisper. "TEMPUS…"

"Okay… Tempus in Latin means time," I said.

"How is your Latin?"

"Not the best. Not the worst," I answered. "As someone said about Shakespeare, I have small Latin and less Greek."

"Do you know the Latin word Itinerantur?"

"If my Catholic school training serves, it means journey."

"Or travel."

"Okay, if you say so."

"Time travel," Luke said as if I should know what he was talking about.

"Luke, I know secrets were your business, but I have no idea what you are talking about. You're being quite dramatic, and it doesn't suit you."

Luke pursed his lips and reached for his water. He drank. He considered. He stared at me. "Remember the Manhattan Project? Do you still have that near photographic memory you used to dazzle us with, Charlotte?"

I closed my eyes and reached back into my memory files. "Top secret group of physicists and government officials who were part of the research and development undertaken during World War II to produce the first nuclear weapons. The first research was based at Columbia University, the University of Chicago and the University of California at Berkeley. Nuclear facilities were built at Oak Ridge, Tennessee and... let me think... yes, Hanford, Washington. The main assembly plant was built at Los Alamos, New Mexico."

I opened my eyes, proud of my still vigorous recall.

Luke grinned, pleased. "Okay, smarty pants, who was the physicist in charge of putting all the pieces together?"

"Easy one. Robert Oppenheimer, professor of physics at the University of California, Berkeley."

"More coffee?" Luke asked.

"Why not?"

After our cups were refilled, and the waitress had

retreated, Luke smiled at me strangely.

"Do you know the name Cyrano Conklin?"

"Never heard of him," I said.

"But you will."

"Okay. Enlighten me."

"Professor of physics at Oxford and MIT. He's in his fifties. He's a genius, which means he's a little nuts. For the last seven years, he and five other physicists have been secretly doing research and development for a thing called the Tempus Project."

"I'm listening."

"They've been working very assiduously on time travel."

I glanced away, shaking my head. "Are you serious? Time travel?"

He jerked a nod. "Very."

I aimed my skeptical eyes at him. "Time travel what?"

He lowered his voice to a near whisper. "They are currently looking for candidates who are willing to undergo testing for possible time travel. In short, I submitted your name."

I stared at him, struggling to read his face. Was this a joke?

"I hear your clever and analytical mind thinking, Charlotte. But it's no joke."

I felt oddly amused, oddly intrigued, and oddly outraged.

"I don't know what to say, but first of all, why didn't you ask me first before submitting my name? I don't know who these people are, what the hell this TEM-

PUS thing is all about and..."

Luke broke in. "... Charlotte, think about it. Just stop and think for a minute. If I had told you, you would have said no... no ifs, ands or buts. Secondly, you fit all the criteria they are looking for."

"And what is that, Luke?" I asked, raising my voice.

He took in a breath. "Brutally honest?"

"Sure, why not? Be brutal."

"You're alone. No family. Few friends. Nothing to live for..."

He threw up a hand to stop me from speaking.

"Your words, Charlotte, not mine. And you have a deep, deep regret and hatred for yourself that you have never been able to shake, not with all the shrinks, the self-help, the booze or even a brief stint with religion."

I blinked fast. I couldn't stop blinking. His words hurt.

"You spent your whole life working for the NSA, Charlotte, working massive hours, being forced by your bosses to take vacations and time off. Now that you're retired, you don't know what to do with yourself, so you drink and read and, I suspect, you are just waiting for death."

"Luke, that's not fair."

"Hear me out. Have you scheduled your bypass surgery yet?"

I stared at him. "No, but that doesn't mean I'm curling up into a ball and waiting for death." I took in a sharp breath and turned my head from him. I was angry. I was scared. I was not able to process the idea of time travel. It was too fantastic. Too out of reach. Too crazy.

Luke reached for my hand and gently squeezed it. "Charlotte... I have had a good life, a fulfilling life: a successful marriage, three great kids, a grandson, and satisfying work. I have watched you struggle for years, unhappy and hurting. I've seen how your guilt has eaten away at you. I was not supposed to know about the Tempus Project. I stumbled onto it through an email error—someone at the NSA mistakenly cc'd me on a memo. Isn't that how wars are won or lost, how dictators fall, and how families are saved? When I read it, I thought of you and I contacted Cyrano Conklin and told him your story. He is very interested."

Luke reached into his shirt pocket, drew out a card and slid it across the table.

"What have you got to lose, Charlotte? What do you have to gain? Just think about it. If there was any possibility that you could return to the past and save your family—no matter how remote and seemingly impossible it seems—how would that change your life? You could spend whatever time you have left watching your daughters grow up. You could see your husband, Paul, alive again and know that you saved them after all. Isn't that worth considering? You may get the second chance that no one else on this Earth has ever been given. You have the chance of getting your family back. Isn't it worth a simple interview with Cyrano Conklin?"

CHAPTER 3

Like many married couples, Paul and I often had variations on the same conversation. I remember this one because it occurred on the morning of Tuesday, June 4, 1968. Steven Case, my boss, had once again asked for volunteers to work late. Politics were highly charged that summer, and the NSA was receiving a barrage of information about possible assassinations. Since the country had gone through three assassinations in less than five years, JFK in November 1963, Malcolm X in February 1965 and Martin Luther King in April 1968, we took the information seriously. There was also new data about possible violent protests at the upcoming Democratic National Convention in Chicago. In addition, we were monitoring the Vietnam peace talks going on in Paris between the U.S. and North Vietnam.

I told Paul that I might have to work until at least eight o'clock.

"Charlotte, the girls were looking forward to having dinner with you. I promised them last night that you'd be home tonight."

"I know it's hard for you, Paul, and I don't want to disappoint them. But at least they'll grow up with a good role model, they'll know that I'm a dedicated professional, that women can perform meaningful and important work and make a difference in this world. When I was growing up that wasn't even a possibility."

"That's all well and good, but we got married so we could also be together and have a family. We talked about balancing work and family."

"Okay, so sometimes the balance is a little off, but that's how things are. Right now, my job requires I give a little more than usual. It will change. I've told you this."

"It hasn't changed, Charlotte. You've been giving more and more to your job and less to the girls."

I got defensive. "I give what I can right now, okay? This is 1968, and things are changing for women. Our lives are finally changing for the better. I just want to be a part of that change."

Paul sighed. "I know you do, Charlotte. All I'm saying is, don't forget us while you're out there changing the world."

"That's not fair, Paul," I shot back harshly. "You know I love you and the girls. You know I'm always here for you if you need me."

Even as I said those words, I anticipated his response.

"Charlotte, honey, you're missing so much of the girls' childhoods, their special moments. Not to mention last week's parent-teacher conferences."

I bristled. "Paul, they're only in preschool."

I lit a cigarette, took a puff and then snuffed it out, folding my arms tightly against my chest.

Paul continued. "But it's important for you to hear how they're doing. And it puts me on the spot. Most of the time I don't know when you're coming home or how late you'll be. It's just that there are times when we all miss you, and that's happening more and more."

"I do what I can do," I snapped. "I have a very responsible job. You have no idea the pressure I'm under, what we're monitoring, between the race riots and the demonstrations against the Vietnam War, which is not going to end any time soon, I can assure you, no matter what the politicians say. I'm working hard to protect our country and make the world a safer place for you and the girls; a better place for everybody."

I laugh at myself now, even as I write those words, those old, arrogant, self-important words.

I secretly knew I was wrong. I knew my family should have come first. No one had twisted my arm to marry Paul, and I was happy to give birth to our two lovely daughters, three-year-old Lacey and five-year-old Lyn. I was selfish. I wanted it all, or, to be blatantly honest, I wanted the status and the respect I got from my job first, and then I gave to my family whatever I had left over, which frankly, wasn't all that much.

Reducing my work hours was something I could have done. I could have worked from nine to five. No one was twisting my arm—none of my bosses. But then everyone was working long hours—the men were working long hours and they weren't seeing their kids either. I had to keep up, didn't I? I was one of the few women in that department. I had the men's respect and I wanted to keep their respect, didn't I?

I could have balanced my work life and my family life. Women do it all the time, now, but I chose not to. I made the choice: me first, and I paid for that choice in the worst possible way.

Many people recall that night in 1968. It was the night Robert Kennedy was shot, assassinated in the Los Angeles Ambassador Hotel a few minutes after midnight, after delivering a speech to his campaign workers. It was an event that dramatically changed the United States if not the world. Being the fourth assassination in the U.S. in five years, it felt as though the country was disintegrating into chaos, and people wondered if our democracy could survive all the violence.

In 1968, I was thin, fit, pretty and, as Steven Case assured me, smart. Many people, including Steven, said I favored the movie star Faye Dunaway, even though I didn't think so.

Although Steven's been dead for nearly thirty years and that night was fifty years ago, I remember him and that night as if it had happened only a week ago. That is my curse. To remember. I have an excellent memory and a sharp mind. I always did. I recall nearly every detail of what happened that terrible night.

On Tuesday evening, June 4, 1968, I left work before six so I could be home for dinner. Paul's arguments that morning had been persuasive, despite my initial defensiveness. We put the girls to bed, drank a few glasses of wine, made love and fell asleep.

At 3:45 in the morning, the phone rang. Stumbling in the dark, I pulled the phone into the hallway in the hopes that Paul and the girls wouldn't wake up.

"Hello?" I whispered.

"Charlotte, it's Steven Case. I just got word that Robert Kennedy's been shot."

"Oh, no."

"I'm asking everyone to come to work as soon as possible. President Johnson wants a report on this ASAP."

I didn't hesitate. "I'll be there in 30 minutes."

I put the receiver down softly and walked quietly back to the bedroom. Paul didn't stir, so I grabbed some clothes, dressed quickly in the bathroom, wrote him a note and softly closed the door.

There was little traffic at four in the morning. I sped down the highway, listening to a local radio station's coverage of the shooting. At 4:30, I walked into Steve's office. He and two colleagues were standing in an alcove adjacent to his office, where the three TV stations (ABC, CBS, and NBC) carried updates on the assassination. All three kept returning to a photo of RFK sprawled on the floor, a busboy named Juan Romero kneeling beside him. Juan had been shaking RFK's hand when he was shot.

We were all visibly shaken. Once again our country's fiber had been torn apart by an assassination, and our intelligence agencies had been unable to prevent it.

The suspect was a Palestinian named Sirhan Sirhan. His motives and affiliations were unknown. Questions filled the room. Would RFK survive the multiple gunshot wounds? What were the ramifications of the shooting for the Democratic party? If RFK survived, would he still be able to secure the nomination and run for president?

Steven finally gave us our assignments and I walked slowly into my office, determined, despite fatigue and depression, to complete my mission.

It must have been 5:35 when Steven knocked on my office door. An unusual silence surrounded him.

"What's wrong?" I asked, jumping up. Something else must have happened.

Steven was tall and thin, with iron-gray hair and black-rimmed glasses. He reminded me of a gentle praying mantis, and if he often gave the appearance of being kind and gentle, he could also be as hard as granite.

He stood next to me, staring down at the floor for a good 30 seconds before he spoke. His expression was grim. "Charlotte," he said, in his proper New England accent. "I've just been notified that there was a fire."

I thought he was referring to our building. But why weren't the alarms ringing? I made a motion to move when he held up the flat of his hand.

"Charlotte, it seems that... well, about an hour ago, I'm afraid your house caught on fire and burned to the ground."

I remember stiffening and glancing down at my watch. It was 5:40 a.m. Why did I glance at my watch? Why did I not react immediately? I'm not sure. In retrospect, I think I was so shocked about RFK that I couldn't shake the mist from my bloodshot eyes and focus on something that seemed a complete impossibility.

"Did you say my house burned down?" I asked, positive I hadn't heard him correctly.

Steven nodded. He reached for my arm, considering his words.

"Charlotte... I am so sorry to have to be the one to tell you. It seems that no one managed to get out of the house before the roof collapsed. The fire inspector who called me said that your family most likely died of smoke inhalation."

My mind couldn't take it in. I kept thinking about time. "What time did the fire start? I mean how..."

"The inspector thinks it started around 4:30. A neighbor called the fire department at 4:43. There will be a complete investigation as to the cause."

Even now, after all those years, I still feel the sharp impact of his words that stab into my heart. I can still feel the coldness grow within me.

My wounded, stricken heart began to pound. Then

it raced, and I felt panicked and lightheaded. I struggled to stay on my feet, lost energy and dropped to a nearby chair, stunned.

Steven was an intellectually aloof man, not a passionate man. He dealt in facts and pragmatics. He was not capable of offering comforting words or arm-around-the-shoulder compassion.

"Are you all right, Charlotte? Do you need anything? Do you have anyone you can stay with? Anyone I can call for you? If you want, I'll book you a room at the Willard Hotel. In any event, I don't think you should drive anywhere. I'll drive you there or call a car service when you're ready to leave."

I stared ahead, not seeing anything. The silence became deafening, my eyes blurry.

"Did you say they're dead, Steven? Are they all dead? My daughters, are they dead? Paul? No, Paul must have gotten them out. He's a light sleeper sometimes. I'm sure he got Lacey and Lyn out of the house. He did, didn't he?"

I looked up at Steven with what must have been pleading eyes. "They did get out, didn't they?"

Steven's eyes searched the room for words, but when they finally settled on me, they were vacant.

"No, Charlotte. From the report I received, Paul and your two daughters died in the fire. I'm afraid they are all dead."

CHAPTER 4

"I'M HERE TO SEE Cyrano Conklin," I told the 20s something receptionist, who had midnight black hair, combed smooth and straight, with small suspicious eyes and lots of frosty reserve. I was impressed.

"Is he expecting you?" she asked.

I stared back at her with equally chilly eyes. "You must be joking," I said flatly. She did not like my manner and she gave me a little arrogant lift of her chin.

I continued. "We both know I would not be here if I didn't have an appointment with him."

We were in a small, close room with a tiled floor, one window that looked out onto a sooty brick wall, one orange reception chair, one mahogany desk holding a laptop, and not one picture on the bare gray walls. The building itself was an old, three-story brick in an old and not so prosperous neighborhood. But it was private and non-distinct and that suited these people just fine, so I learned later.

The receptionist pouted a little. "Even if you have an appointment to see Mr. Conklin, he may not see you, depending on his schedule. He is not a man who is..." she searched for the right word, while I waited with rapt curiosity. "He sometimes forgets things," the receptionist concluded. "May I have your name, please?"

I looked at this young woman and softened. I didn't need to be rude. After all, she could have been my granddaughter, if my daughters had lived.

"My name is Charlotte Vance."

"Thank you, Ms. Vance."

Minutes later, I was buzzed into a quiet square room containing an open brick wall with a boarded-up window, three gray walls, same color as reception, one card table with a chair, and one uncomfortable looking high-backed wooden chair. The receptionist asked me to sit in the high-backed chair facing the card table, saying Mr. Conklin would be with me as soon as he could.

I sat, glancing about, feeling the rise of nerves. Again, there were no adornments on the walls, and I noticed a second door to my right. I figured Mr. Conklin would appear from that door, and about ten minutes later, he did.

Cyrano Conklin was a stout, broad man with a square face and a humorous expression. Even the dimple in his chin appeared humorous. He was probably in his mid-50s, and his eyes twinkled with a boyish friendliness. His pug nose seemed all wrong for his face. His messy grayish hair was thinning on top but long on the sides, and he wore a rumpled brown corduroy coat, loose fitted jeans, and a denim shirt. He also wore sandals with no socks.

"Well, well, Ms. Charlotte Vance, I am indeed happy to meet you," he said, with an outstretched hand and in a British accent.

I was on my feet, taken by his enthusiasm and warm greeting. He pumped my hand with gusto and asked me to sit. He rounded the card table and sat behind it, his folded hands resting upon it, an easy smile relaxing me.

"Quite a room, isn't it?" he said, glancing about. "No frills. It's the kind of room I imagine police detectives would use when grilling a suspect. Don't you think so, Ms. Vance?"

It seemed an odd thing to say. Still, I nodded and answered, "Yes."

"But, of course, we don't have that damn blinding light glaring in your face like they used in those old 1930s and 1940s cop movies, do we? So, not to worry," he said with a chuckle.

I didn't know what to say, so I said nothing.

"Now, I have heard a lot about you, Ms. Vance."

"You can call me Charlotte, Mr. Conklin," I said, trying to appear calm, although I was anything but. What I was there for was something so unbelievable and so extraordinary that I had difficulty relaxing. I gently twisted my hands.

"Okay, then you must call me Cyrano. Can you imagine the ribbing I took at Eton College when I was a boy, Ms. Vance? What a name, Cyrano. What a silly revealing name, huh? My father gave it to me because he said when I was born, my nose was so small, he hoped my name would help make the little pug thing grow. Well, there you go, Ms. Vance. My father was a bit of an eccentric as you can readily see. A brilliant scientist, yes, but also a bit out of touch with the real world, if you know what I mean. Well, then look at me now. Many say the same thing about me, don't they, Charlotte? Well, I mean to say, look at what I'm involved in here. Time Travel. Who would have believed such a thing? Did you know that I was going to study classics at Oxford, Charlotte?"

"No... And you didn't?"

Cyrano leaned back and stared up at the ceiling as if his past were on display up there. "Literae Humaniores, the study of the literature, history, philosophy, languages and archaeology of the ancient Greek and Roman worlds. Yes, Charlotte, I was keen to study the classics. Somehow, I wound up at Cambridge University studying physics. Well, who would have thought such a thing? Did you know, Charlotte, that by 1642 the study of physics became required at Cambridge?"

"No, I didn't."

"Well, after that, I was off to MIT and into things I never thought I'd fall into. But I did fall into things, and here I am. And here you are, Charlotte."

Cyrano rearranged his mood. He turned serious, focused. His eyes narrowed, and he stared at me in a hypnotic way. I couldn't pull my eyes from his.

When he next spoke, his voice was deeper, and filled with conviction. "Charlotte, I was captivated by your story. I was moved by your story. To be completely direct, I am enthusiastic about the possibilities of your time traveling back to 1968."

I stared, feeling my eyes widen. He'd spoken so matter-of-factly, so casually, as if time travel involved nothing more than booking a flight to Europe. It electrified me. I trembled, and my eyes stung with tears, startled by his declaration and the storm of emotions his words provoked.

I struggled to speak, but the words choked in my throat. I tried again. "Can it be done, Cyrano? Is it truly possible to time travel? You hear so many things these days. Most of what I've read says it can't be done, at least not in the way we think. Is it possible?"

Cyrano closed his eyes and pinched the bridge of his nose. "Charlotte, I am a scientist who believes in practical magic."

"Magic?" I answered, again taken aback by his words.

"Practical magic," he stressed, with a pointed finger. "Yes, because the entire world is made up of a kind of magic. We simply have to learn to speak the language of magic. Now, some of that language is mathematics and some of that language concerns quantum mechanics, but a very important component of that magic concerns a mystical word called intent."

"Intent?" I asked, not comprehending, knowing I sounded like an echo.

"Yes, Charlotte, but all that will come later. Right now, be assured that time travel is possible. I will confide in you this much: we have proved that time travel is possible because we have accomplished it on a small scale."

He looked into remote distances. "Our first experiments were simple ones. We once sent a cat named Missy back into time—two days. We clipped her nails before we sent her, and when we went to retrieve her, her nails had not been clipped. We had also used a kind of atomic clock that proved the cat had indeed traveled back in time."

He smiled broadly. "As you can imagine, we have come a long way since then, and we are ready to take the next large step."

Cyrano paused, stood up and laced his hands behind his head. "You are here, Charlotte, because I believe you may be the right person to time travel into the past, in your case, back to 1968."

I stared hard, feeling as though I were talking to an alien. "Time travel..." was all I could say, in a tart, skeptical voice.

Cyrano eased back down in his chair, measuring me.

"I wasn't going to explain much to you until we completed some tests, but I'm going to let you in on a few things. I think you deserve that. Charlotte, as difficult as it may be for you to believe, we have discovered that we live in a digital universe; that is, we are truly made up of bites and bits or 1s and 0s, just like bites and bits on a hard drive in a computer. We are like animated avatars in a computer game. At the quantum level, Charlotte, the world is less defined than a simple yes and no, or 1s and 0s. We do not live in a deterministic universe as Newton believed. We live in a probabilistic one. In other words, we can manipulate future probabilities with our intent. Intent being a very important and necessary element. Also, since we are essentially digital, and the universe is informational and digital, we can move ourselves around—if one learns the practical magic—the same way we move around things on a computer desktop."

Cyrano paused, gathering his thoughts.

"So, you've already sent others back in time?" I asked, struggling to comprehend.

He shook his head. "We have sent a cat named Tiger back in time, and a dog named Spot. The problem is, we are not so sure we placed them in the time and place we were aiming for, and we were not able to bring them back. Simply and frankly put, we don't know where they are or where they went."

He smiled, meekly, opening his hands. "You see our problem?"

"But what about the first cat? The one you sent back for two days?"

"Ah, yes. Well, you see, the clock has limitations and our technical device had to be, shall we say, expanded and, with the expansion came our discovery of intent."

I looked at him pointedly. "So, what you need is a human to add the final component: intent."

"Exactly, Charlotte. Well thought out. You have grasped the so-called ungraspable very quickly. I'm impressed."

I wasn't flattered. I was worried, even scared, seeing that this man firmly believed in what he was saying.

I sat up a little straighter and adjusted my shoulders. "So, let's get to the bare-bones truth of this, Cyrano. What you need is someone who has already lived her life, has a weak heart, has few friends and family, and who desperately wants to travel back in time to save the family that perished in a fire in June 1968. You need somebody like me, who has nothing else to lose by taking a chance—a wild and, frankly, crazy chance that could very well kill her. A chance that she may never be heard from again. But that's okay, because no one will miss her. And, anyway, if she is killed, she should have died long ago in that burning house with her family."

Cyrano ran a hand across his face. When he looked at me, his eyes held warmth and understanding.

"We want this time travel adventure to be a win-win for all of us, Charlotte."

Diplomatic, I thought. "Forgive me if I'm not especially optimistic, although, as I implied, what do I have to lose?"

Cyrano fixed his serious eyes on me. "Charlotte, have you ever heard of Lord Kelvin?"

"No."

"He was a British mathematician and physicist. Very well-known and respected in his day. In 1895, he said heavier-than-air flying machines were impossible."

CHAPTER 5

Having worked for a government agency until my retirement at seventy, I can say with some experience and confidence that many government agencies are staffed by dedicated, hardworking and patriotic people. But they are, like many families and most organizations, sometimes dysfunctional, territorial and disorganized. Nearly all are incapable of achieving the herculean feats that most conspiracy theorists and spy novelists suggest.

Luke said TEMPUS is the exception. It is run by six or seven front people—I'm not entirely sure of the exact number, and there are more who work behind the scenes. They are a close, secret, highly intelligent, fiercely loyal and territorial group. Luke mentioned that the President and Vice President of the United States, along with most senators, know nothing about TEMPUS, which I found a bit alarming. Funding comes from private money and money siphoned away from two other secret organizations, which I will not disclose.

I met Cyrano Conklin again a week after our first meeting, at the same location, and this time I met the rest of the six-person front team. First was Alex Mason, a 30-year-old physicist who wore a blue t-shirt and khakis and had auburn boot-camp short hair and the youthful expression of a smartass know-it-all. He was muscular and well built, looking more like a warrior than a physicist. He was also quite handsome, in a dangerous sort of way.

Next was Maggie Greer, a 35-year-old computer programmer specializing in Nano technology, who had a tight cap of red curly hair and big, red-framed glasses that she was constantly adjusting.

Walter Sieg was a tall, taciturn Swiss mathematician and computer programmer, who always seemed lost in thought or contemplating other worlds in the great beyond.

Dieter Krauss, a 38-year-old German physicist and historian, had spiked blond hair, very blue eyes and a formal, no-nonsense manner.

The final member of the team was Kim Stein, a 45-year-old psychiatrist and "consciousness expert," whose gentle smile made me both irritable and nervous.

We sat in a conference room containing only an oval conference table, one window covered by a brown curtain, a coffee maker and, interestingly enough, an old pinball machine that worked. Alex Mason played the thing, working the flippers and "dinging" the bells as the rest of us spoke.

"By the way," Alex said, glancing my way with a roguish, lopsided grin, "this pinball machine is from 1968. I found it on *eBay*."

Cyrano facilitated the meeting and everyone but Alex was seated around the table in various states of curiosity and calculation. Laptops were out, and cell phones were at the ready.

Cyrano seemed relaxed and focused, giving me encouraging and earnest attention.

"Charlotte, all of us here today are just the forward and visible part of a much larger team of theoretical physicists, practical physicists, mathematicians and, for lack of a better term, psychics."

I tried to present a passive face, but I'm sure my eyes expanded when he said psychics.

"Before we can proceed further, Charlotte, we will need for you to undergo a battery of tests: physical, physiological, emotional and mental. Frankly, we are concerned about your heart. I see from the medical records you forwarded to us that you have coronary heart disease."

I remained silent.

"And there are other issues we must address. We want you to be aware of all the risks of undergoing this time travel experiment."

I was seated at the far end of the table with an untouched bottle of water before me, as well as a sheet of paper which I assumed was a confidentiality agreement of some kind. I must have looked grave and concerned, and I was. It was intimidating and disconcerting to be sitting there while these geniuses studied me, clicking away at their laptops, assessing every word and movement I made.

"But before we get into all that, we have a very important request to ask you."

I waited.

"Charlotte, if this doesn't work out—that is, if for whatever reason we feel you are unsuited for this, shall we say, little experiment, we must ask you to keep TEMPUS, and everything that goes on here, and everyone you have met here, a guarded secret. We strongly request that you sign the statement on the table in front of you, simply as a friendly formality."

I felt mildly insulted. I sat up a little more erect and tried not to sound too imperious.

"I will sign your form, Mr. Conklin, but let me point out that I worked for the NSA for many years and, in all that time, I was privy to more secrets about this country, its people and its leaders—not to mention the past leaders of this world—than most of you, if not all of you, will ever see in your collective lifetimes. I assure you, I can keep a secret."

I saw a little smile crease Cyrano's lips. Alex stopped playing his pinball game long enough to shoot me a humorous glance.

Kim Stein, a very thin woman with large, startling dark eyes, and her entire left arm covered by tattoos, also smiled and gave a little nod of approval.

"Well said, Charlotte," Cyrano said. "Well said, indeed. And, of course, that is one of the reasons we selected you for this project. I'm sorry I have to ask, but

I'm sure you understand."

"Yes, I understand. May I ask if you are interviewing other candidates?"

Cyrano's face seemed suddenly to button up. "I'm sorry, Charlotte, I am not at liberty to say. I'm sure you understand, once having worked in intelligence."

I nodded, feeling a sudden rise of steely determination. I had always had a strong competitive spirit, and now I was hell-bent on being the chosen candidate.

"I know you told me you'd sent a cat and a dog back in time, but have you ever sent a human being?"

The scientists shifted in their seats, their eyes glued to their laptop screens.

"I'm afraid I can't tell you that either, Charlotte."

I offered a weak smile.

From their collective reactions, or lack thereof, I was sure they had, indeed, sent a human being back in time, or at least they had tried. I felt a new twist of discomfort.

Cyrano clasped his hands together. "Well, then, I think we can proceed with the testing, if you are in agreement, Charlotte?"

CHAPTER 6

The tests were grueling and long, but it was the physical I dreaded the most, afraid my heart condition would quickly eliminate me. It was conducted by a 40-something, no-nonsense woman who explained things methodically and unemotionally, in a strictly professional manner. That was okay by me.

The stress test was called the Dobutamine-Atropine Nuclear Stress Test, and the entire procedure took a couple of days. On the second visit, I entered a cardiac testing lab and was given medication to make my heart temporarily beat harder and faster while a dose of radioactive tracer was given. After the stress portion of the test was completed, I was placed under a nuclear camera for heart pictures. A couple of times, I thought my pounding heart was going to jump out of my chest.

I spent a few sleepless nights and long, anxious

days, waiting to hear from Cyrano. After a week had passed and still, no one had called, I despaired. Being desperate and uncharacteristically emotional, I drove to the three-story red brick building intending to burst inside and plead for another chance. Fortunately, I did not go in and I drove on, struggling to settle my mind.

It was a Sunday morning in early March when I finally received a call from Cyrano.

"Charlotte, so good to hear your voice again."

My heart was thumping against my ribs, and I willed it to relax. I stood staring out my window into a clear sunny day. In the distance, I could see the Washington Monument.

"I thought you weren't going to call," I said, immediately wishing I hadn't said it. I was trembling and my voice shaky.

"We had much to consider and much work to do. But I have good news. We'd like you to come in for another meeting."

"Another meeting? You mean I still haven't been chosen?"

Cyrano's voice was calm and measured. "We must be patient, careful and methodical. We must be certain that this project is as safe as possible for you, and as successful as possible for all of us. We have spent years and a lot of money to get where we are today."

I heaved out a sigh, turning away from the window. "Of course. I'm sorry. I've just been on pins and needles these last weeks, waiting."

"I know. Yes, I know Charlotte. Can you come in tomorrow, Monday morning, at 9am? You will be meeting with Kim Stein."

"Yes, of course. I'll be there."

"And Charlotte, I'm going to tell you something I shouldn't. I am pushing very hard for you, but we have a few more hurdles to overcome. Nonetheless, I am confident we can surmount anything that comes our way. All right, then. I'll see you tomorrow."

Kim's small office was tidy and almost cozy compared with the other TEMPUS rooms I'd been allowed in. A vase of fresh flowers sat on her desk, as well as a gold framed color photo of a man in his forties and two children, a boy about twelve and a girl about ten. The photo had been taken in autumn under a blaze of red and orange leaves. Black framed professional-style photos of various types of trees hung on the walls.

Kim was an attractive woman with large wondering eyes that especially caught my attention. Her medium length dark hair was combed back smoothly from her forehead, revealing silver hoop earrings. She wore a navy blouse, skinny jeans and heels.

I sat in a comfortable black leather chair across from Kim, who sat behind her desk.

"I love trees," Kim said. "Ever since I was a girl, they've captivated me."

"Did you take the photos?" I asked.

"Yes," Kim said, turning to look at them and point. "Those are a Lombardy poplar, a birch, and a Cyprus tree I took in Italy. The one near the window is a 120-

year-old oak tree I found in San Antonio."

"It's even older than I am," I said, lightly.

Kim faced me with a warm smile. "Charlotte, I'm going to come right to the point. We are very concerned about the condition of your heart. I'm sure that is not a surprise to you."

My shoulders slumped, and I lowered my gaze. "No..."

"In your heart's current condition, we cannot take the chance of sending you back in time."

I lifted my eyes, feeling myself wilt. "So that's it then..." I said resigned.

"No, that's just the bad news. The good news is you are going to make your heart stronger, and I am going to help you."

I looked at her, not comprehending.

"Charlotte, I am what some people would call a psychic, but I'm actually more than that. I'm officially known as a consciousness expert. Simply put, I believe in mind over matter because I've seen it work and I have used it myself with success. I was affiliated for a time with the Princeton Engineering Anomalies Research lab, also called the PEAR lab. It was a research program at Princeton University that studied parapsychology."

"I have heard of the PEAR lab," I said.

"Simply put, Charlotte, you and I are going to spend the next few weeks and maybe months working on two things. Improving your heart and strengthening your intent."

"What does intent have to do with it?"

Kim sat back in her chair. "Without a strong intent, no one can time travel or even enter altered states of consciousness for any amount of time. Wishing to go to the past or the future will not work. It's too weak. Even willing it, intellectually, and trying to manipulate it technologically, will not work. But a quiet mind and a strong intention—that is, an intention that comes from your very being, your very core of who you are—will work, in conjunction with the technology that we will be using."

I thought about this, still unable to grasp the totality of what Kim was saying.

Kim stood. "Charlotte, what makes you a strong candidate for our project is that your intention is solid and authentic, and it has been building since 1968. You deeply feel a desire to fix the perceived wrong that occurred to you back in 1968. All that remains for us to do is to quiet your mind and strengthen that intention, so you can focus and hold it for the quantity of time it will take us to send you back into time."

My hands were clammy, thoughts racing. "What do you mean, hold it?"

Kim eased back down in her chair, allowing some silence to gather her thoughts.

"We live in a probabilistic universe. Quantum mechanics has proven that. When we move you into the realm of the quantum world, which is where you'll be for a time, your intention will be the most powerful tool to guide you and finally take you back to June 1968."

I sat blinking and staring.

"Are you comfortable working with me on this?"

I nodded. "Yes… Yes, whatever it takes."

"You will stop drinking any alcohol or caffeine. I suggest a vegetarian diet. Also, I'm going to teach you how to meditate and you will do so twice a day for forty-five minutes. We must start quieting your mind, erasing the usual static of thoughts and fears, so you can focus on healing your heart."

"Should I continue taking my heart medication?" I asked.

"Yes, absolutely. We don't want any new shocks to your system. We want you to relax and grow stronger."

The meditation, intention focus, and vegetarian diet all sounded like absolute nonsense to me. It was so New Age, strange and esoteric, but I was willing to do whatever it took to return to 1968 and make better choices for myself and my family.

"Are you okay with all this?"

I nodded, exhaling. "Sure… Yes."

Kim smiled, reassuringly. "It will be fun, Charlotte. You will experience a whole new you, and I think you will enjoy the process. So, shall we begin?"

CHAPTER 7

On July 6th, I had my second stress test, conducted by the same doctor as before. As I looked at myself in the mirror that day, I marveled at the change in my appearance. My skin was smoother, its color improved; my eyes were clearer; my hair a glossy, soft blonde with subtle silver highlights, cut in a shorter hairstyle suggested by Kim. I'd gained muscle tone. My balance had improved. I'd been sleeping better than I had in years. All in all, I felt stronger and calmer than I had ever felt in my entire life.

I had followed Kim's exercise, diet and meditation regimen faithfully for almost four months, as well as practicing my mind/body and intention exercises religiously.

It remained to be seen if my heart would pass the last test that would determine if I'd be allowed to move to the final phase of preparation for a time travel journey back to 1968.

A week after the stress test, I was invited to meet the entire team back in the conference room. As I entered, I was met by Cyrano, who had a broad, welcoming smile on his face. Although I was calmer than during our first meeting, I still felt a ripple of apprehension as I sat down at the oval table. I quickly looked to Kim for support and was relieved to see her reassuring, sunny smile.

The other members were professionally friendly, while Alex, the pinball wizard (as I had silently labeled him) was sitting angled in his chair, staring into his laptop.

Cyrano ceremoniously clasped his hands as he often did before beginning.

"Welcome, Charlotte. I must say that you look wonderfully relaxed and healthy and I have heard great things about you over the last few weeks. How do you feel?"

"I feel great," I said, feeling like a prep school applicant hoping to impress the school board.

"Excellent. Well, let's get right to it. We have processed all of your tests and we are pleased."

I almost leapt from my chair. "So I passed the stress test?" I asked, blurting it out.

Kim smiled, and I noticed that Alex smiled as well. I sensed that a smile from him was a rare thing.

"There is a significant improvement."

I didn't like the sound of that. I waited for more. "What does that mean, Cyrano?"

"Although we'd hoped for a better showing, your heart has strengthened enough that we are now confident that we can proceed to the next steps."

On triumphant impulse, I clapped my hands, feeling the start of joyful tears.

To my surprise, the entire team applauded me, and then they applauded Kim. I joined their applause of her.

When the room fell into a pulsing silence, Cyrano fixed his solemn gaze on me.

"Charlotte, I have wonderful news. You have been selected to time travel back to 1968."

I couldn't stop the flow of tears. Both Dieter Krauss, the German physicist and historian, and Maggie Greer, the wizard programmer, handed me tissues.

After the emotion wore itself out, I thanked everyone for standing by me and selecting me.

Maggie spoke up first. "Charlotte, now is the time for you to ask us any questions you may have. I'm sure you have formed many over the last few months."

"Yes, Charlotte," Cyrano said. "Feel free to ask us anything."

I folded my hands and slowly looked each one in the eyes, closely fixing them in my mind.

"Forgive me for asking this question, and please don't feel insulted, but do you truly believe you can send me back in time to 1968? In the last few months I have done a lot of research, reading everything I can get my hands on about time travel. The theories of special and general relativity do allow for it, but the serious literature and articles I have read state that time travel to the future is much more likely than time travel to the past."

There was a long silence. It was Dieter who spoke first, and while he spoke, Alex arose and went to the pinball machine.

"Charlotte... All of us have spent most of our lives in service to science. We routinely sacrifice our relationships with family and friends, and work long hours, often seven days a week, solely for one purpose: to focus all our energies on stretching the possibilities of science, hoping to make real and practical all the theoretical aspects of science. It is our lives—and yes, we do believe we can successfully send you back to June 1968, or we would not attempt it."

I fixed my hard stare on Dieter. "Maybe you are all fools," I said.

There was another icy silence. Alex stopped playing and glanced over. As the silence lengthened, Alex shut down the pinball machine and drifted back to the table, taking his seat to my left. All were staring at me, puzzled.

"There is an irony here," I said, finally breaking the silence. "Back in 1968, I gave up everything for *my* work, and I lost my family to a tragic and senseless fire. I should have been there with them that night and, who knows, if I had been there, I might have been able to save them. If I couldn't have saved them, then I should have died with them."

I reached for a bottle of water and took a drink.

"Now, here I am all these years later, willing to risk my life, or what there is left of it, to return to the past, to change the past and change it because I did exactly what you people are doing now: I lived to work, and worked to live, and to hell with everything else, family included. Forgive me if I sound direct and rude. I don't mean to be. I am so thankful to you all for this opportunity, I just hope you listen to an old woman, and don't make the same mistakes she made."

I paused to take another drink. "Of course, the further irony is that it is your obsession with science that may allow me to atone for my past. Mine was a sin of omission and not commission, but it was a sin, nonetheless. I did not set the fire, but I failed to cherish my family as I should have. Now I want to atone for that sin if I can. I not only *want* to go back to 1968, but I *must* go back, to save my family and to save myself. If I don't, I know my suffering will never end. And so I thank you all again for your willingness to live the way I did, even as I encourage you to learn from my mistakes."

There was another long, heavy silence as all eyes were lowered on the tabletop.

I inhaled a breath, realizing I had said too much. But it had to be said. I had to get it all out one last time.

"Now, about those questions," I said. "I do have some."

CHAPTER 8

The scientists sat in an uneasy stillness, waiting for my questions.

"If I go back to 1968, will I be the age I am now, seventy-six years old, or will I be twenty-six years old, the age I was then?"

Walter Sieg, the Swiss physicist, spoke up. "Theoretically, you will be seventy-six years old."

"Theoretically?" I asked, amused.

He shrugged. "None of our models reveal there will be any change in age, but of course you will continue aging in 1968. You will leave here at seventy-six years old and you will arrive in the past at seventy-six years old. The real challenge for us is to make sure you land within weeks of your target date of June 5, 1968. We will program you to land sometime in late May: the 23rd, 24th or 25th. That will give you plenty of time to rest and recover and then complete your mission."

"If I successfully go back to 1968, and if I manage to save my family and they survive, won't that change the world as we know it? My daughters' lives could possibly change the entire course of the world, couldn't they? Theoretically, they or my husband could do something that could even destroy the world. I mean, I know it sounds overly dramatic, but it is possible, isn't it?"

Alex drummed an impatient single finger on the table. "Yeah, well, it's the age-old time travel question, isn't it? I've heard this question so many times that, frankly, it just bores me. I mean, who cares if three—forgive me here—if three nobodies live instead of die and live out the rest of their lives? It's simple, isn't it?"

"Not to me, Alex," I said. "It's not simple, and it is not theoretical. It is not just an experiment or a video game where you and your scientist friends will gain points and win the game. They were my family."

Cyrano spoke up, but Alex held up his hand to stop him. "I'm sorry, Charlotte, I didn't mean to offend you. All I'm saying is that if you successfully return to 1968 and can save your daughters and husband, they will undoubtedly change the world. Of course. There's no way around it. They will grow and make choices that will affect their lives and many people's lives, and yes, they will change the course of events of this world. The questions are, one, will they be quality changes, and, two, so what?"

"So what?" I asked.

"Yes, being your daughters, and assuming you'll raise them to be good and ethical citizens of the world, they might change the world for the better, don't you think? Look around, Charlotte. Is the world so mature and enlightened? Listen to the news every day. We're a race of whining babies, slinging sand at each other in a sand box. Let's face it, and you know this better than most of us, the world is a fucked up and volatile place. Instead of making this world worse, maybe your daughters will improve it—especially if you can successfully convince your younger self who you are, where you came from and why you came. You, Charlotte, are a quality person who will have a lot of quality power over your younger self, your husband and your daughters."

I sat entranced, impressed by Alex's words. I hadn't thought of this. I looked at Alex as if I were seeing him for the first time; that young, confident warrior face and cool intelligent eyes. He suddenly reminded me of a boy I knew back in the early 1960s, who got into drugs in San Francisco and died from an overdose.

I paused. "So there will be two of me back there, in1968? The 76-year-old me and the 26-year-old me?"

Alex slowly nodded. "Yes. And there's more, Charlotte."

Cyrano stood and held up a hand to stop Alex. "There is one important aspect about all this that we haven't spoken of since our first conversation many months ago. Now is the time we must share this with you."

I felt sweat trickling down my back. "Okay, fine, I'm ready."

Cyrano folded his hands and looked at his colleagues solemnly before his eyes came to rest uneasily on me.

"Although we have struggled to solve this last problem—an important problem—we have run into barriers and, for now, we have abandoned it, focusing all our energies on the business of what we can realistically achieve. Well, let me just come out with it. If we succeed in sending you back to 1968, we don't have the skill, the technology nor the knowledge to bring you home, that is forward, to this time. You will have to finish your life, whatever your natural lifespan may be, back in 1968."

I shut my eyes and took in a breath. "I see. So, I will be another kind of Laika."

"I beg your pardon," Cyrano said. "I'm afraid I don't know who Laika is."

I opened my eyes, casting them around the table. "I'm sure your resident historian, Dieter Krauss, knows who Laika was, don't you Dieter?"

Dieter nodded, with some pride. He straightened in his chair.

"Laika was the first dog in space, and the first creature to orbit the Earth. Laika was launched by the Russians on a one-way trip on board Sputnik 2 in November 1957, and she died in orbit about a week after the launch."

Every head was down, eyes staring into laptops.

CHAPTER 9

I sat up straighter, hoping to display courage. "It's okay, really," I said. "I'll make the best of my two lives: the young woman and the old woman. I suspected this some time ago, but I'd still hoped I would be coming back home to the present. Now that I'm not, I will have to prepare mentally for that: the old me and the young me, living in the same time. And if I'm successful in my mission, I'll have to keep my distance from my family. It's a lot to take in, and it's weird and perplexing."

Cyrano leveled his earnest eyes on me. "Do you still want to go through with it?"

"Of course I do," I said without any hesitation. "Don't all of you?"

They lifted their heads, nodding, but avoiding my eyes.

"I have another obvious question. You have all worked so hard on sending me back in time, but why not just send one of you? Why go to all the trouble, heart condition and all, of sending me?"

Kim raised her eyes to me. "I believe we answered that question some time ago, Charlotte. We all volunteered to time travel. We wanted to, especially Alex. Yes, we all wanted to very much, but we learned over the course of much trial and error and experimentation that we lacked the one crucial element that you possess naturally and fundamentally: Intention. That terrible event in 1968 has owned you and defined you. Losing your family in that fire is embedded in your being and so tattooed on your soul that in conjunction with our technological help, we have every reasonable confidence that you have the best chance of any other candidate of having a successful time travel experience. Finally, you lived in 1968. You recall the look and the feel and the smells. These are all the many reasons we strongly believe you will successfully time travel to the past."

I leaned back and let that sink in, as another question formed. "But the cat and dog went back in time. They presumably had no intention."

The corners of Cyrano's mouth lifted in a smile, but it was Alex who spoke up.

"You are quite perceptive, Charlotte. All of us here are first and foremost committed to this project because we want to make the world a better place. By going back in time and fixing some of the, let's say, flaws of the past, perhaps we can improve the present and the future. If we have the means and skills, why not?"

Cyrano took over. "What Alex is getting at is what you and I discussed some weeks ago. We need realistic and measurable goals. The cat and dog had no intention and, therefore, they also had no measurable or definable location on the grid. They traveled willy-nilly. In other words, we could send them back in time, but without an intention we had no idea where they landed: perhaps in the Atlantic Ocean in 1850; or an alley in London in 1776; or in Antarctica 2000 years ago. You see, Charlotte, intention is the key. It is the invaluable device, albeit somewhat mystical, that must be present, so we can target and then measure our success."

I waited, staring and thinking. I examined all their faces and saw conviction and agreement.

"Okay, then. I have two final questions. First, can you tell me, in layman's terms, because I don't know much about physics or quantum mechanics, or time travel, how you discovered the key to time travel?"

Cyrano looked at Alex. "I will let Alex explain that."

Alex stood, went behind his chair and placed his hands on the back, inclining toward me. His eyes were cool and direct.

"To put it in laywoman's terms," he said, with a smart little smile, "I hacked into the universal computer system."

I stared, not comprehending.

"By accident, really, I found that codes, like computer codes, are a fundamental aspect of nature. Mathematical structures of super-symmetric representation suggested to me that we are living in a very sophisticated computer. Behind the scenes of the binary-code world we live in, there are many more modified and specialized minor codes operating, camouflaged under a bunch of misleadingly clunky old binary facades."

"I'm sorry, you've lost me," I said.

"Okay, simply put, Charlotte, I found a kind of back door into the entire universal computer system that allowed me to manipulate movement and space/time through certain mathematical formulas, codes and space/time models, with the help and focus of the power of intention. Think of your desktop computer. You can move folders and files around, right?"

I nodded.

"That's what we plan to do with you. We will move you from the 2018 folder on a kind of desktop to the 1968 folder on another part of that desktop."

The room was quiet. They were all waiting for my reaction. I simply didn't know what to say.

Walter Sieg spoke. "Charlotte, reality is not what we think it is or what our senses report back to us. It's strange and wild, and contradictory. True reality is hidden beneath everyday experience, and its inner workings are even weirder than the idea that something can come from nothing and return to nothing."

I nodded, but I didn't really understand, and a part of me didn't care. If they could send me back in time, then fine. That's all that mattered.

Alex nodded toward Kim. "With Dr. Stein's help, you now know what intention is, Charlotte, and you have practiced and learned how to apply your intention. That will be of prime importance as you guide yourself back to 1968, with the help of our computer codes and formulas, of course. We call it a merging of space/time and mind/body, if you will. Does that help answer your question?"

I looked at him blankly. "Thank you, Alex. I'm afraid I'm not a very technical person… at least not in that way."

Alex shrugged and sat back down.

I continued. "My last question is this. If I can't return to the present from the past, then how will all of you know if your time travel experiment was a success? How will you measure it? You won't know if I survived, or if I landed in 1968, or 1779, or died."

Cyrano brightened. "Great question, Charlotte. An excellent question. This is much easier to explain than all that quantum stuff. The answer is both simple and challenging. This will all be riding on your very capable shoulders. What you must do is convince your younger self the truth of what we've done here—that we have successfully sent you back in time. Then you must further convince your younger self that when she is seventy-six years old in 2018, she must come to us here at TEMPUS and tell us everything that transpired in the last fifty years."

The words hung in the air as I struggled to process all the information. I saw several nodding heads, as if Cyrano's answer were straightforward and self-evident.

I swallowed. "That seems very speculative and tenuous," I said.

Cyrano nodded, spreading his hands in agreement. "It's the best we can do at this time, Charlotte, and the best we can hope for."

"And what if my younger self doesn't believe me? Because I can tell you that I know myself, that 26-year-old self, very well, and I would not believe the crazy ramblings of some 76-year-old woman who told me she was my older self who just happened to drop in from the future. I would run from her and call the police. Look, if I can get back there, I know I can save my family from the fire, but I'm not so sure I can convince my younger self that time travel is real and that you people exist and are anxiously waiting for her to appear before you in 2018."

No one was smiling. No one was looking at me.

Cyrano got up. "Charlotte… maybe you'll have to contact your husband. Maybe he'll believe you even if your younger self doesn't. Maybe he'll convince his wife. At the very least, you should be able to convince him to leave the house with your daughters on the night of the fire."

"Yes, I will do that as a last resort, of course. But the further reason I want to return to 1968 is to change 26-year-old Charlotte. If she only hears about Paul saving my daughters, *she* won't have the experience —that personal and necessary experience that will change her, because she nearly lost her family. I need her to *want* to change her life, and convince her that if she doesn't change, her life will be wasted, family or no family. You see, I want her to come out of this whole thing a wiser and better person."

Cyrano looked toward the ceiling as if seeking an answer. "It's a lot to ask of yourself, Charlotte."

I felt that my head was about to explode. "Yes, I suppose it is, but I've had a lot of sleepless nights thinking about it. It's okay. It's fine. I'll find a way to make it work, one way or the other. I just want to get on with all this. When do I go?"

CHAPTER 10

I had a little over a month to prepare. The target date for my time traveling back to 1968 was set for Friday, May 25, 2018 at 3 a.m. Predawn was the most favorable time for time travel.

I'd already taken care of my finances. I'd updated my will, giving generously to charities such as the American Red Cross, Doctors without Borders and Amnesty International. I also left money to women I knew who were divorced and struggling to raise their kids, as well as to students I'd met who were heavily in debt. It gave me a good, uplifting feeling. If I didn't survive my time travel ordeal, at least I could feel I'd done something good with my life, no matter how small.

I sold my condo and my car, arranging to transfer ownership after I had left, and gave all my good clothes and shoes to Goodwill, along with furniture and household objects that still had value. A friend had said I'd feel a strange satisfaction and uneasy peace when I tossed out old clothes, dishes, furniture, magazines, books and newspapers. She was right.

It felt as though a part of me was dying, and I suppose that was true. I *was* dying—perhaps literally, perhaps only to this time. But, yes, it would be a death, one way or the other.

I still couldn't entirely get used to the idea of time traveling, and there were still times when I felt foolish and silly for even considering it. How did I really feel about death and dying? Kim Stein had asked me about this some weeks ago. I said, "I feel like a part of me died a long time ago."

The hardest part of tossing out years of accumulated stuff was going through my closets. I had not yet dealt with the photo album of my family, a 3-ring binder with three plastic sleeves per page that had somehow survived the fire. There were three photos in it.

On the morning of Wednesday, May 23, I knew I could no longer procrastinate. I wilted a little in depression when I removed the old album from the back shelf of the closet and took it into the kitchen. I sat on one of the two stools still at the kitchen counter, not moving for a time. It took strength and courage to open the thing, as the old familiar dread filled me up. But I finally opened it and ventured a look at the first page—the only page with photos

A sharp pain cut my heart, I slammed the album shut and instinctively grabbed at my chest. "Throw the thing in the garbage like you should have done years ago," I said aloud.

Outside, I removed the top lid of the green garbage can. I was just about to drop the album inside when I stopped. On impulse, I quickly opened it and ripped one plastic sleeve containing a single faded color photo of the four of us and, without looking, I slipped it into my back jeans pocket.

I decided to take it with me, back to 1968. I don't know why. It was a sentimental family photo, taken during our last winter together. Paul, the girls and I were standing outside the house in the snow, all bundled up in red and white ski hats and heavy coats. Paul held the girls aloft, one in each arm, showing off his strength in a playful way. He'd told the girls he was as strong as Superman. They'd laughed and told him he was silly.

Three-year-old Lacey had chocolate brown hair, was fussy, curious and liked coloring books. Five-year-old Lyn had blonde curls, loved her Giggles doll with the orange dress, and seldom missed the children's show *Captain Kangaroo*. I'd often thought how much the girls would have loved *Sesame Street*.

With tentative eyes, I studied Paul. Dear Paul had been the prime homemaker. Long before it was common for men to do so, he had cooked and cleaned and taken care of the girls. When his job grew more demanding, he hired Florence Ambrose, the matronly housekeeper and babysitter, who was a godsend.

I stared at the photo, trying to understand the woman I had been then. Our next-door neighbor, Doris Scully, had snapped it. At that time, she was the age I am now. She had no kids of her own and her husband was dead. She'd been a dear, sweet and lonely woman.

After she'd snapped the photo, the girls and Paul had built a snowman and then Doris had invited them over for hot chocolate. I heard all about it later because I had left them to go to work. What a stupid woman I had been.

The only other item I would take with me to the past was my grandfather's gold pocket watch. He'd been my favorite person when I was growing up and he'd loved me unconditionally. On my thirteenth birthday, a few months before he died, he pressed the watch into my hand and said, "Charlotte, keep the watch and remember me. It is my wish and God's certainty that it will always protect you." I often wore it to work, and I had done so on the day of the fire. It was one of the few objects from my past that I still owned.

△△△

THAT NIGHT, Luke Baker, who had been following my progress with TEMPUS since he first introduced me to the organization months ago, brought a pizza over for a farewell dinner. No beer was allowed. I would need a clear head the next night as I created my intention for time travel.

We sat on the two stools in my empty kitchen, searching for things to say.

"I will miss you, Charlotte."

I looked at him and saw by his tender expression that he meant it. "What a nice thing to say. You've been my only real friend, and a good friend. Hey, I wouldn't be doing this if it weren't for you."

"Yeah, I've thought about that. It is something you truly want, isn't it, Charlotte?"

I nodded. "Yes... Very much."

"Are you scared?"

"Yes. Sometimes at night, when I can't sleep—which is most nights now—I actually find myself praying to a God I'm not sure I even believe in, pleading my case that He or She will allow me to go back so that I can truly change my past and somehow make a difference in this world."

"You know that you were one of the best analysts the NSA ever had."

"That's much ado about nothing, Luke. In what really mattered, I failed. I've lived all alone in a narrow little world I created for myself. I tried to move on, but I couldn't."

Luke stared at me kindly, taking my hand and squeezing it. "Okay, Charlotte, so now you will have your chance."

My eyes welled up. "Yes. I hope you'll say a prayer for me."

"I'm not much of a praying man, but maybe God will lean my way just this once and hear my special prayer for you and your family."

At the front door we hugged, and then he was gone. I turned back to my shell of a home and walked the empty rooms, hearing the echo of my footsteps, sounding like the tick, tick of a clock. I was scared. I was scared to death.

CHAPTER 11

On Thursday, May 24, less than twenty-four hours before I was to time travel, Cyrano ushered me into the Launch Room, as it was humorously called. It was an L-shaped room on the first floor with no windows. They'd been bricked up. The room contained glass-topped desks with four desktop computers and six 34 inch curved LED monitors. The blue LED strip lighting that ran along the ceiling was muted, and the eerie glow from the monitors created a futuristic type atmosphere, not a retro one.

There was a single chair placed against an open brick wall—a kind of soft black leather recliner, the same I'd used with Kim during my first meditation training sessions. I was happy to see it—an old friend. But the slender seven-foot-tall obelisk that stood next to the chair was truly captivating. I couldn't pull my eyes from it, staring into it with a fascinated wonder.

Waves of blue and white light shimmered and flashed through a smoky reddish fog.

I pointed at it. "What is that?" I asked Cyrano.

"A kind of cosmic computer."

Alex, Maggie, Walter, Kim and Dieter were all present, seated or stooped behind the monitors, absorbed and whispering, as if mumbling incantations. The mood was somber, although Cyrano tried for smiles and an upbeat manner. I tried on my 1968 outfit. I'd be wearing a simple light blue dress that was sleek but loose, because I would be carrying $60,000 of hidden cash from 1968. I do not know where they had managed to get cash from 1968, and I didn't want to know. A light cotton white jacket and black pumps finished the look.

My fashion expert was Wynter Albrecht, a tall willowy blonde of about forty, who was also a physicist. (Wasn't everybody at TEMPUS?)

Wynter was absorbed in animated thoughts and gestures, speaking glibly, as if she were lecturing a freshmen college class.

"By 1968, the psychedelic style had burst onto the fashion world with all kinds of weird dresses and tunics, bell-bottom jeans, tie-dye shirts and miniskirts. These bold, casual fashion statements were, in themselves, a rebellion and a protest. They stunned and startled a conservative world that had held fast to the suit and tie, the elegant dress, with matching hat and white gloves. This consensus uniform had lasted for generations, but almost overnight, it was discarded, and our culture was completely transformed, to the casual dress of today."

I gave Wynter a pointed look. "I remember the 1960s well, Wynter. I was there."

She glanced up, a bit startled. "Oh, well yes, of course you were. Forgive me, Charlotte. Anyway, at seventy-six years old, you wouldn't be a part of that rebellious generation, so that's why I dressed you in the earlier style."

I was carrying some of the $60,000 in hidden cloth pockets sewn into the dress. The remainder was in my purse and in a sleek money belt concealed under the dress.

Cyrano and Dieter came by, handing me my 1968 driver's license and passport. My new identity was Charlotte Wilson, born in Chicago, Illinois.

I didn't have to worry about credit cards. It wasn't until the 1970s that women could even have credit cards in their own name.

Later, we all sat in the conference room, feeling the strain of the approaching day. Dieter's eyes were alert and active, as if calculations were going off behind those tired eyes. Alex did not play the pinball machine. He seemed uncharacteristically distracted. Maggie worked constantly on her laptop and Kim, as always, smiled pleasantly. Walter Sieg was not present.

And then came the most emotional moment. The final consent form awaited my signature. Part of it read:

The Purpose of the Experiment

Why I was a Candidate
Other Factors

And then finally:

```
I understand that the risks involved can
be life threatening, including stroke,
brain damage, loss of mental function
and death.

Having read (or had read to me) and
having understood all the above, I do
hereby voluntarily consent to partici
pate in this "physics experiment" and,
in no way, hold TEMPUS, or any employees
of TEMPUS, responsible for the outcome
of said experiment, whether successful
or unsuccessful.
```

I did not hesitate to sign the form. I'd committed myself to the physics experiment weeks ago.

Finally, I signed another form making Cyrano my legal caregiver. If I developed brain damage, or had to be placed on life support, I did not want to be kept alive. I instructed Cyrano to "pull the plug."

In the event of my death, TEMPUS would secretly take care of my burial. I would be buried at Oak Hill Cemetery with my family, in a plot I'd purchased in 1970.

At the end of a very long day, Cyrano and I were alone in his office. I saw the dark circles around his eyes and noticed that he'd aged noticeably in the last few months. We'd become good friends, if not close ones. Long ago I'd stopped making friends, and I'd forgotten how. Luke had been my last.

From across his desk, Cyrano slipped a typed piece of paper toward me, with six companies' names and their corresponding stock ticker symbols.

"Charlotte, as you know, the $60,000 you're taking with you is worth about $400,000 by the standards of 1968. When you arrive, contact a broker and invest $45,000 into those six stocks in equal proportions. Keep $15,000 in a bank account. That's about $100,000 for that time. If you live to be eighty-two, the investments from those six companies will make you a millionaire."

He grinned ruefully. "Time travel has its advantages, but it has made me a crook."

I stared at the paper and tried for a kind of joke. "I always wanted to be a millionaire."

Cyrano exhaled a soft breath of finality. "Well, Charlotte. Are you ready?"

"Yes... of course."

"I will miss you."

His genuine kindness touched me. "Really?"

"Yes. I will wait anxiously for your return."

"But it won't be me. If all this hocus-pocus works, when I return, I will be someone else."

Cyrano lowered his eyes. "Maybe something wonderful will happen tomorrow. I hope so, and I believe so."

Our eyes met, and his were misty. "Charlotte, I wish I could go with you."

I hesitated, a thought rising. "I never thought to

ask. Do you have regrets, Cyrano? Do you have things in the past you wish you could change?"

I saw a tender sadness in his eyes. "Oh, yes, Charlotte. Oh yes…"

PART 2

CHAPTER 12

In the Launch Room, I sat in the deep, comfy leather chair, leaned back and tried to relax. It wasn't easy. My heart was kicking in my chest. I was sure my blood pressure was rocketing up. Not good for a person who was supposed to be in a tranquil state, so her mind could form an intention of returning to 1968. My heart pills were sewn into a pocket, not that I could take one now, and a vintage 1960s suitcase was on my right. No one was sure that the suitcase would travel. "Stop thinking so much," I told myself.

Kim stood over me, smiling her usual reassuring smile. "Just allow yourself to relax. There's no rush. You're about to begin a new adventure, so begin by taking deep breaths and letting them out slowly, just as we practiced."

I did so, but my pulse was high, and my mind was a tangled mess.

I ran through my instructions again—for the thousandth time. I heard Cyrano's instructions in my head.

"Charlotte, in 1968, this building was a school textbook distribution warehouse, not unlike the Texas schoolbook repository warehouse that was involved in the assassination of President Kennedy. We have sorted through all the blueprints of this building and have positioned you to land in 1968, on the first floor, just before dawn on May 25th. No one will be in the building at that time. We did our historical research. The first shift begins at 8 a.m. You will stand and walk out of the room and turn right. Down the hallway and to your right you'll see a side exit door. We are positive it is not alarmed. Push the door open and enter the world of 1968."

Kim's voice startled me back to the present. "Close your eyes and allow your thoughts to settle, Charlotte. Breathe easy and begin counting your breaths… Breathe in, breathe out, one. Breathe in, breathe out, two."

My thoughts continued to race. "I bet they regret having chosen me for this," I thought. "Am I too old? Why did they think a woman my age could do this? Why did I agree to this? I'm seventy-six years old, for God's sake! I was a terrible choice. The wrong choice."

As I fought for calm, I caught sight of Alex staring at me intensely. He stood near the obelisk of blue light, and he was bathed in it, little sparks of light circling his body. I'd never seen that before.

More thoughts cut in. "Will I be dead soon? What if I wind up in another time—the 1800s or even before that? Stone age? What if I wind up in the future and the world has been blown to bits? What will I do then? What if I'm the last person alive on the Earth? What the hell good would that suitcase do me?"

Again, Kim drew me back to the present. "Relax, Charlotte, and imagine the little house by the sea we created. It's quiet, there are flowering gardens and you can hear the soft hiss of the waves as they roll up on the beach. Just relax now. Relax and breathe easy."

I kept breathing.

"Feel the energy slowly build in your hands and feet," Kim said soothingly, nearly at a whisper. "Feel your heartbeat soften and relax."

I don't know how much time passed before the agitation of my mind slowly dissipated, but Kim was gone, and the room seemed to be on the periphery of my mind. I heard a soft electric buzzing sound. Gradually, I began to drift down into a quiet pool of darkness, sinking beneath the surface static of my thoughts, down and down, into the depths of scintillating blue light. Here, now, I was to form my intention, in this soft blue light. First, I repeated my intention to myself several times. "Return to May 25, 1968 in safety and peace."

Next came the visual image of Paul and my daughters—the three of them before me—as they'd appeared in that winter photograph. They were smiling and calling, willing me to return to them with wiggling fingers.

I held the image, firmly, as I had been trained. It had taken weeks of practice to hold this image steady, with no mental movement, no intruding thoughts, no chaotic emotions or extraneous images. Only Paul, Lacey and Lyn were fixed on the screen of my mind. In time, I saw them waving at me, calling for me to come to them, their voices sounding like distant echoes.

Time must have passed, but I had a sense of pulsing timelessness. And then, I was startled by distant voices, mumbling. I felt a cold draft of wind wash over my face; the sound of the sea, its waves thundering toward the beach, crashing, thudding onto shore.

I mentally held onto my image—even when my heart felt a stabbing pain that nearly snatched the precious faces of my little girls from my mental grasp. No... No, I held on, feeling my body vibrate and shake. Still I held on, not with the force of strength, but with the firm authority of intention, anchored deep in that peaceful, endless ocean. Fear charged and attacked. My body felt as though it were breaking into pieces— arms reaching, legs wide, head spinning. Was I going to be pulled apart?

I heard bells—distant church bells—Christmas bells? A choir singing. More agitated voices. I heard shouting, and a rumbling explosion somewhere off in the distance. Running water. Wind chimes. Laughter. I heard shouting crowds, and the growl of airplane motors roaring over my head.

Suddenly, I was flung into a sharp cold wind—sailing, whirling helplessly over mountains and moonlit lakes, geese racing by, clouds whipping past my face.

Darkness and light. Darkness and light. Bitter cold. Icy, bitter cold. Still my tenacious mind held fast to my daughters' faces, to Paul's sparkling blue eyes, to the sound of his smooth baritone voice. Intention: Return to May 1968 in safety and peace.

Then something slapped at me—wind? I felt a punch in the gut. Air exploded from my mouth. My heart drummed, ached, pounded. I couldn't hold consciousness. I began to slip away into a tunnel of darkness—an endless tunnel—tossed and hurled into cavernous depths, arms flailing, heart feeling as if it would explode.

This is it, I thought. It's over. I'm dying.

CHAPTER 13

A slow pulsing. Pain in my chest. Head pounding. Can't move. Can't be dead. Too much pain. Darkness. Distant siren. Where?

Floor... hard. Cold. On my side, I think. Moved my foot. Pain. Moved right hand. Am I in shock? More pain. Heart hurts. God how it drums in my ears. Mind is numb. Thoughts seem frozen, like glaciers. Can't think. Can't reason. Cold. Where am I?

My entire body was a throbbing bruise and I couldn't move it. A slow creeping panic began to rise. I felt helpless, vulnerable and, as my consciousness slowly began to awaken, I struggled to open my eyes. Darkness. Heaviness.

It was the pain in my heart that prodded me to roll over on my back, like some helpless turtle. I grimaced in pain and reached, with a straining effort, for the pocket that held my heart medication. Had to get it.

I walked my stiff fingers to the spot, worked to peel back the Velcro, and probe the pocket for the flat case that held the pills. No! No… Paste. The pills were just a paste. The case was a mass of goo. Again, I fought panic. Stay calm, Charlotte. Stay calm.

I touched the paste with the tip of a finger and brought it to my mouth. I did this several times, each time taking easy, careful breaths, until my heartbeat settled and the shock of impact subsided.

It was imperative I find out where I was, so I could make some decisions. With all my strength, I rolled over onto my stomach and, with my hands, strained to push up to my knees. My entire body was shaking, and my pulse was much too high. "Can't die, Charlotte," I whispered. "Not now. Can't die here."

Minutes later I was on my feet, leaning precariously against something. A box? I crabbed my way along what felt to be a row of boxes until, high above, I saw the dim glow of light streaming through a grimy upper window. I squinted, feeling like a prisoner in a dungeon, desperate for freedom. Yes, it was light! Daylight. Hope added needed strength. I stayed put, letting the strength build as the light brightened. Dawn?

As darkness gave way to gray shapes and sizes, I glanced at rows of cardboard boxes stacked against the walls. I searched for my suitcase. Nothing. It wasn't there. It didn't make it. My nervous eyes darted about, looking for my purse. I saw it on the floor and felt a flood of relief.

My thoughts began to thaw and flow. Okay. Good.

Next. Had I landed in the right place at the right time, Saturday, May 25, 1968 at around dawn? I reached for my grandfather's gold stopwatch, which I had tucked securely in another sewn pocket. I felt for it. It was there. I opened the pocket and carefully drew it out into the murky light.

My shoulders sank. The face was cracked, the hands frozen at 4:12 a.m. I held it to my ear. No sound. I heaved out a sigh and returned the watch to my pocket. The broken watch blunted my morale. Was it a sign that I'd fail my mission? I recalled my grandfather's words as he lay dying. "Charlotte, keep the watch and remember me. It is my wish and God's certainty that it will always protect you."

With great effort, I managed to retrieve my purse and then stand for a time to gather much needed strength and balance. As my eyes adjusted to the light, I saw a closed door. My heart fluttered, pains shooting through it. I doubled over in agony and had to wait until the pain subsided.

Standing stoically erect, inhaling deep breaths, I didn't stir, afraid I might shatter into pieces. Minutes later, I finally mustered the courage to make a move. I wobbled over to the door, praying it wouldn't be locked. If it was locked, I'd be caught by some warehouse employee and no doubt held until the police arrived to question me. Cyrano and I had gone over just such a scenario and I was ready with my answers, but I was in no physical shape to go through any kind of interview. I had to get out in the air, so I could breathe. I was terrified that I would have a heart attack and die right there.

My palms were sweaty when I reached for the doorknob. I gripped it, swallowed and turned. Thank God it opened into a long narrow hallway, just as the TEMPUS team had said it would.

I shut my eyes in deep relief. This meant, at least for now, that I had arrived at the book warehouse precisely where I was supposed to land. The next question was: had I arrived in the right year and on the right date?

I shuffled down the dim, silent hallway, passing dark offices with glass doors and stacks of boxes shoved up against the walls, my hand sliding along the wall for support. My breath was labored. Where was that exit door? I had to find that door and get outside. I knew if I could just get outside, I'd be okay.

Just ahead, I saw it. On the right. An EXIT sign and a gray metal door only a few feet ahead. And then, out of the corner of my eye, I saw something move. I froze. I looked left. There was an office enclosed in glass. Seated inside the lighted office window, peering out, was a man, his face pinched in surprise and alarm.

Fear burned my face. I willed myself erect as he sprang out of his chair, rounded his desk and entered the hallway. He wore a short sleeve white shirt, dark tie and dark slacks. His steel-gray flattop haircut and black-rimmed glasses made him appear militaristic.

He put fists to his hips, narrowed his suspicious eyes, and then glanced up and down the hallway to see if anyone was with me.

"Can I help you, ma'am?" he asked, frostily.

I gave him an innocent, grandmotherly smile. "How are you this morning?"

"Well, I'm fine. What are you doing here? How did you get in here?"

I used my rehearsed lines. "Perhaps you can help me. I'm lost."

"Lost?"

"Yes… I'm looking for Mr. Wilson?"

"Wilson? I don't know of any Wilson," he said.

"Well, I'm sure he works here."

The man seemed perplexed, which is just what was expected. My goal was to deflect him from suspecting me of anything and then fall on his sympathy.

"Ma'am, nobody will be working here for another two hours. It's only five o'clock in the morning. Now, I am Seymour Haynes, the security manager. Is there something I can help you with?"

I acted flustered. "Well, I don't know. I was supposed to meet my grandson around here someplace."

"Ma'am, how did you get in this building? All the doors are locked. I checked them all just an hour ago, and I can assure you that all the doors, and I mean all, are locked."

I managed a kind smile. "Well, they can't all be locked if I walked in, can they?"

I'd put him on the defensive. Now, I had to get out of there.

"You'll have to excuse me, Mr. Haynes," I continued. "Obviously, I have entered the wrong building. I'll just go now and try to find my grandson."

Thankfully, Mr. Haynes decided to drop his guard and become chivalrous. "Is there anything I can help you with?"

"No, no..." And then I had an idea. Why not turn this to my advantage?

As I turned to exit the side door, I looked back at Mr. Haynes.

"Mr. Haynes, forgive me, but what month and day is it?"

Mr. Haynes relaxed, his eyes registering understanding. My act had worked. He thought, "*This old woman is senile and confused, and she needs my help.*"

He cleared his throat. "It's Thursday, May 30, 1968. Are you sure I can't call someone for you?"

What had he said? Thursday, May 30, 1968. But I was supposed to land on Saturday, May 25th. No, it couldn't be. I was supposed to have plenty of time to rest, to contact my younger self and persuade her not to leave her family alone the night of June 4th. I would need all that time and maybe more.

Mr. Haynes noticed my sudden alarm. I must have turned snow white. "Are you okay, ma'am? Can I call you a cab?"

I stared at him, not seeing him, my mind reeling.

"Ma'am... are you feeling alright?"

I turned from him, pushed open the side door and blundered out into the humid, soft pearl light of Thursday, May 30, 1968.

CHAPTER 14

The door slammed behind me as I staggered outside. The world flooded in, jarring and bright, and I shaded my eyes with a hand, almost falling. Grasping a wrought-iron railing, I descended two concrete steps, struggled across the sidewalk and leaned against a parked car. The heart pain returned, and I winced, gasping for air. Cyrano had instructed me to rest for several days after I'd landed, warning that my body would need to settle. From the deep, aching fatigue I felt, I'd be lucky to make it through one day. I needed my medication. I needed something to sustain me, to strengthen me.

I heard Kim Stein's voice. "Relax and breathe, Charlotte. Take everything step by step. Don't get ahead of yourself. Don't force. Don't push. Allow things to unfold and then calculate your choices. Many things may not work out according to plan. Be patient and calm. Tell your heart to relax."

How could I accomplish all I had to do in six days? As I stood there panting, squinting up into the brightening sky, I didn't feel properly anchored in my skin. It was as though pieces of me were still scattered and hovering somewhere, lost, searching for the totality of me.

I don't know how long I stood there, besieged with pain and doubt, taking deep breaths, my head bowed, my eyes shut. When I heard footsteps, I lifted my blurry gaze. A middle-aged woman with gray hair and bifocals moved closer.

"Are you okay?" she asked softly.

"Just a little dizzy," I said, blinking, forcing a weak smile.

She was wearing a light pink summer suit and low heels. "Are you alone? Is someone close by to help you?"

I struggled to speak.

"Do you have a car nearby?"

"No..."

"Are you waiting for someone?"

"No..."

She stared at me, confused.

In a strained, whispering voice, I said, "I don't know. I think I was waiting for someone..."

The woman glanced about, her mind active. She examined my face and clothes in speculation.

"My office is right over there," she said finally, pointing. "Why don't you come with me and I'll call you a cab. Can you make it that far?"

I could have said no, but I didn't want the police

cruising by. If Mr. Haynes had seen me stumble onto the sidewalk and lean against a parked car, he might have called them.

"Thank you," I said. She offered me her arm, and we slowly made our way through the parking lot toward her office. Not far from the door of the building, pain shot through my chest and I stopped, bending forward.

Just then, a car drew up and stopped. The driver rolled down his window.

"Do you ladies need some help?" he asked.

I peered through slitted eyes. He was a silver-haired man in his late sixties, with a pleasant face and a concerned expression.

"This woman is faint. I offered to take her to my office and call a cab."

The man emerged from his car. "There's a hospital nearby. I can take her there."

My head felt as heavy as a bowling ball, but I managed to lift it. His voice was soft and kind.

"No, no. I don't need a hospital. I just need a cab. I need a ride to the Willard Hotel."

"I'll take you there."

I blinked, not sure what to do. "Are you certain it's not out of your way?"

"No, no. I'd be happy to drive you there."

Mechanically, I turned by head, facing the woman. She nodded encouragement.

I turned back to the man. "Do you know where it is?" I asked.

"Sure. Pennsylvania Avenue."

"Well then, I'd be grateful."

"Thank you for your help," I said to the woman. She still held my arm at the elbow.

"I hope you feel better," she said, releasing it.

I stepped forward.

"Do you need a hand?" the man asked, noticing I faltered.

"Yes, I'm afraid I do."

He took my outstretched hand and carefully ushered me toward his car, a light blue Chevy Belair four-door sedan. He opened the passenger door and lowered me into the seat, closing the door behind me. I'd never felt so frail and old and alone. Had I aged when I returned to the past? How ironic that would be.

I waved a final goodbye to the woman and then massaged my tired eyes as we lurched ahead, moving into early morning traffic.

"I hope I'm not taking you away from anything," I said.

"No, no. I was just on my way to meet a couple of friends for breakfast. They can talk your arm off. They won't miss me. By the way, I'm Jay Anderson."

"Charlotte Wilson."

"Feeling better?"

"Yes, some."

"Are you from out of town?"

"Yes and no."

"A mysterious woman," he said going for a little joke. "I like mysterious women."

My energy was nearly gone, and all I wanted to do

was lie back and go to sleep, but I was afraid that if I closed my eyes, I would die. I decided to ask questions to help me stay awake. "What do you do, Jay?"

"I'm retired. I was in the construction business. My company helped build the Woodward and Lothrop department store, and the Arena Stage, among others."

"Sounds like you liked your job."

"Yes, I did like it. And what about you, Charlotte? Are you still working?"

I looked at him. He had a lined face—the face of a man who had worked hard in his life, but it was a good face; a trusting face.

"I worked for the government."

Jay laughed. "Nothing like narrowing it down there, Charlotte. Most of Washington, D.C. works for the government."

I smiled a little, feeling stronger now that I was seated. I looked out the window, eagerly taking in the streets, the cars, the people and their dress. To see 1968 again was a surreal experience, and I was excited, confused and nervous. The edges of everything seemed too bright and too sharp, as if my eyes had not quite adjusted to it. My emotions felt like a turgid sea, rolling, splashing, thundering toward shore.

"Are you sure you're feeling all right, Charlotte?" Jay asked, softly.

I snapped back to the present. "Yes... I'm sorry. I guess I was lost in thought. What were you saying?"

"You said you worked for the government and I said that most of Washington works for the government."

I struggled to focus on the conversation. My mind

was blunted and dull, my body sore, my heart drumming.

"It was secret work, Jay, and it was a long time ago."

"Do you have family around here?" Jay asked.

I shivered a little. That's right. If the world is as it should be in 1968, then my family is here. Now. They're alive, and they are here. And I'm here. How weird and bewildering. How wonderful and impossible.

Jay must have sensed my sudden change of mood. "Did I say something wrong, Charlotte?"

"No. It's just been a long night—a very, very, long night."

"Been traveling?"

I laughed. "Yes. I have definitely been traveling."

I noticed that Jay took a few wrong turns, but I didn't say anything since I was enjoying the scenery. As we came to the corner of New York Avenue and 15th Street, NW, I glanced out to see the old Savings and Trust Company Bank, which in 2018 is the Sun Trust Building. I've always loved the Queen Anne-style red brick, with its distinctive gold-domed corner turret and clock. I smiled, recalling that in this time, 1968, I bank there. I have money in there or, to be more accurate, my younger self has money in there. The thought gave me a ripple of goose bumps. I'd be meeting her soon. Me, as I was in 1968. What an incredible thought. What an absurd thought. What a frightening thought.

Jay turned onto F Street NW and drew up to the curb of the Willard Hotel, with its four welcoming Ionic columns.

"Well, here we are."

He ducked down and stared at the hotel entrance. "Too rich for my blood, Charlotte. Do you have a reservation?"

"No... I'll have to throw myself on their mercy."

"No suitcase?"

"No..."

Jay looked me over, curiously. "Fast trip, I would guess."

I nodded, not looking at him. "I hope so."

"Do you want me to help you inside?"

I had a sudden idea. Time was short, and my energy was low. I'd have to move fast, and I realized that Jay might be a godsend.

"Jay... I was wondering... I was wondering if you'd be free to drive me around while I'm here. Just a few days. I'll pay you well. Very well, in cash. I know this sounds a little crazy, coming from a perfect stranger, but I have some things I need to do and very little time to do them in."

Jay shrugged, amiably, smiling broadly. "Of course. Why not? You just say where, Charlotte, and old reliable Jay will take you there."

"That's very kind of you. We can work around any previous commitments you might have."

Jay placed his hands on the top of the steering wheel, turning reflective. "My kids are grown and gone, and my wife, Sally Ann, died two years ago. Do you know how bored I get with nothing to do? I'd be happy to be your chauffeur."

I smiled at him in gratitude. "Thank you so much for helping me back there."

I reached into my purse and took out a 20-dollar bill. I handed it to him.

He stared at it, puzzled. "What's that?"

"That's for you. That's for helping out an old woman in distress."

"Stop it with the old woman, okay? If you don't mind me saying so, you're a very attractive woman, Charlotte. I can see that you have class and character."

His sincere compliment touched me, and I nearly choked up with emotion. It wasn't like me, but then, I had changed over the last few months.

"Please take the money, Jay."

"Put your money away. Hey, old Jay is always good for a helping hand. If you want to give me a little something later on, fine, but not for this. This I did because I wanted to do it, okay? Don't insult me."

Reluctantly, I returned the money to my wallet. "You're a very nice man, Jay. Thank you."

"Stop it, Charlotte. What the hell are we living for if we don't help out people now and then? You got a pen and paper? Something to write on?"

I searched my purse, but I didn't have either paper or pen. Jay found paper and pencil in his glove compartment and scribbled down his name and telephone number. He handed it to me.

"Day or night, Charlotte. I'm a lonely man with a lot of time on his hands, and I'm not so happy about what's on TV these days... Except for *Gunsmoke* and the late movie shows. I love the westerns with Gary

Cooper, Jimmy Stewart and Kirk Douglas. Last night I watched *Last Train to Gun Hill*. That's one helluva good western. Do you like westerns?"

I smiled, warmly, gratefully. "Yes, Jay, I do."

He jerked a nod. "Good. So maybe sometime you and me will watch a western together."

I liked Jay. I liked his kind and open energy. "I think that would be fun."

"Okay, well, let me help you into the hotel. I see the Porter standing there looking at us, wondering if we're coming or going. I've always wanted to climb those limestone stairs, enter that lobby and walk across that red carpet."

"If you don't mind, Jay, I'll go in alone. Another time?"

I looked away from his disappointed eyes.

"All right, Charlotte. I'll take you up on that."

CHAPTER 15

Inside my hotel room, I collapsed onto my queen-sized bed and fell into a deep sleep. When I awoke, I was spooked and panting for breath. It took a few frantic seconds before I realized where I was and what time I was living in. It was 2 p.m. on Thursday May 30th. I had so many things to do. So many things to think about.

In my dozing stupor, I glanced about for my cell phone then remembered I didn't have one. Of course I didn't have one. This was 1968. No cell phones. No PCs or laptops. No voice-activated devices, no cable, no streaming and no *Uber*. Well, Jay Anderson had agreed to be my *Uber*, hadn't he? What a stroke of luck that had been. I hoped my luck would hold out.

I needed clothes. There was no overnight delivery in this time. Okay, what did we used to do? First, I called room service and ordered a club sandwich and a pot of coffee. Then I dialed the Concierge, a man named Oliver, and asked if he could arrange for someone to shop at the nearest department store and buy me some clothes.

He assured me that that would not be a problem. The hotel would purchase my items on hotel credit. I would forward cash to the front desk and that would be applied to the overall cost when the clothes arrived.

I gave him my order and sizes for lingerie, two simple but fashionable dresses—colors green, navy blue or rust brown—and two pairs of shoes, one with low heels. I added two pairs of slacks and two matching cotton tops.

When the bellhop knocked on my door, I handed him a sealed envelope containing 700 dollars, sure that would easily cover the cost, being somewhere in the neighborhood of $4000 in 2018. A few minutes later, Oliver called to say he'd have my order delivered to my room by six o'clock that evening.

After I ate the sandwich and drank two cups of the delicious hot coffee, the first cups I'd had in months, I stood up slowly, testing my legs, pacing the room, discouraged that the dizziness had not entirely passed. My legs were steadier, but I worried about my erratic pulse. With no heart medication, I speculated about seeing a doctor. Did I have time? If the tests were negative, would he insist I spend some time in the hospital? No time for that.

In the luxurious bathroom with its thick, fluffy towels and roomy shower, I washed my hair and lingered under the warm spray, hoping to wash away fatigue, doubt and worry. Afterwards, I belted on the white terry robe provided by the hotel, sat on the bed and stared down at the phone.

I recalled all the old phone numbers: my number at the NSA; Paul's work number at Marion Ad Agency, and our home number. I longed to hear Lacey's and Lyn's voices—I longed to confirm that they were there, and alive. But when I reached for the receiver, my hand trembled and I couldn't pick it up.

Where would they be now? Lacey would be watching TV or playing with her dolls. Lyn would probably be coloring. The housekeeper, Florence Ambrose, would be with them. She was strict but kind, and the girls liked her. I hung my head. Paul had found her, not me. I hardly knew her. Yes, Paul had always been the reliable and steady one. The girls had worshiped him.

I sat there frozen. If I called home, Florence wouldn't let a stranger talk to the girls. If I called Paul, what would I say? If I called myself at the NSA, what would I say? I mustn't raise any suspicion.

I stared at the walls, arms crossed. Of course I had a plan. Cyrano and I had planned everything—including contingency plans—but all of that had been theory and possibility. That had been in another time and another place. Now that I was here—now that *this* time was my reality—I was terrified, and my pulse remained high and driving.

△△△

My clothes arrived at 5:30, and although only one of the dresses fit, a heather-tone low-waisted dress made of acrylic and rayon, the shoes miraculously fit, the lingerie was fine, and the slacks and tops would do. I'd finish my shopping tomorrow.

Bolstered by my new wardrobe, I called Jay Anderson. He picked up on the third ring.

"How about dinner?" I asked. "By the way, this is Charlotte Wilson."

"Charlotte," he said with surprised enthusiasm. "Good to hear from you."

"So how about it? Are you hungry? Dinner on me and I won't take no for an answer."

"I've never been asked out by a woman before," he answered.

"It's 1968, Jay. Things are changing. Don't you listen to Bob Dylan?"

"Bob who?"

"Never mind. If you drive, I'm buying."

"Where are you taking me?"

"To the Baltimore Delicatessen, at 1101 Bladensburg Road NE."

"I know that place. They have great corned beef sandwiches."

Yes, I thought. And my younger self loved to eat there after work. I'd searched my memory and recalled everything I'd done that week. On Thursday night, May 30th, the 26-year-old me had eaten at the Baltimore Delicatessen. It was time I met her. I had to get things moving even though I had a lump in my throat and a kicking heart.

"What time?" Jay asked.

"As long as we're there by eight."

Silence. "Are you meeting someone there?"

"I hope so, Jay. I certainly hope so."

CHAPTER 16

The Baltimore Delicatessen was casual, crowded and boiling with energy. Jay entered first, and I followed, tentatively, amazed by the cigarette smoke that hung in the air like a stringy fog. I'd forgotten about that—about how much nearly everyone smoked—including me. I'd kicked the habit in 1982. I was also startled by the women's hairstyles: beehives, flips, swirls and curls of hair, sprayed into place like fine sculptures.

There were some young men with long hair and beards; some in lace tunic hippie shirts or floral striped shirts, and the young women with them also had long, loose hair, floral tunics and bell-bottom jeans. In contrast, the businessmen still wore dark suits, white shirts and dark ties, and had closely cropped haircuts.

My eyes darted about, looking for her—looking for me. I glanced at my watch. It was only 7:30. My face was hot, my pulse high. I'd never felt such sharp anxiety.

Jay found a table near the front window that looked out onto the street, and I sat, exhaling a deep, grateful breath to be off my feet.

"Are you feeling all right?" Jay asked. "You look pale."

I managed a tight smile. "Yes. Just a little hungry."

"Do you see the person you're looking for?"

"No... not yet."

He glanced about. "It's crowded. Maybe they're already here, somewhere."

"No..."

"Take a look again, Charlotte. It's easy to miss people in this place."

"They're not here," I snapped.

Jay shrank a little, as he slid a bowl of dill pickles my way.

"I'm sorry, Jay... I guess I'm just nervous."

"And you're hungry. I always get irritable when I'm hungry. My wife used to say I was as mean as a bear if we didn't eat right when I got home at six o'clock on the dot. Have a pickle. They're the best in the city."

The thought of eating anything made me nauseous. I kept hearing Cyrano's words repeating in my head.

"Be sure you rest the first couple of days you're there, Charlotte. You must rest. Our past experiments have shown that it takes time for the body to adjust and sync itself to any new time."

I felt exhausted and unsettled, but what could I do? I had to work fast. I'd lost a full week.

The waitress arrived in a hectic flush. I ordered the first thing I saw—sturgeon scrambled with eggs and onions. Jay ordered the corned beef sandwich.

Fortunately, I'd have a good view of the table where my younger self would sit with her friend, Angie. The table was occupied now by a young couple, locked in intense conversation: political, no doubt. This was a famous spot for White House interns, staffers, congressmen and the occasional senator.

Jay glanced about, his disapproving eyes falling on the hippies. "I wonder how many of those are war protesters or draft dodgers," he said with disgust. "Kids today want to protest everything. Nothing is good enough for them. According to them, our generation messed up the world. Where were they in World War II?"

I was only half listening, distracted and riddled with anxiety. I still didn't entirely believe I had time traveled, and the thought that the younger me would come walking in and sit down at that nearby table utterly terrified me.

Kim and I had worked on techniques to minimize the shock and stress of this very event. Kim had told me it would be one of the most traumatic things I would ever experience.

"Slow down your breath, Charlotte, and silently keep repeating 'Relax... relax.'"

While Jay chattered on, I applied my instructions, but fear built upon fear. Would she recognize me? Would I recognize her? Would my old heart give out despite the deep breathing? My pulse was galloping.

At ten minutes to eight, our food arrived. Jay ate voraciously while I kept checking my watch.

"Go ahead, Charlotte, eat. You said you were hungry."

I pushed around the eggs and managed to swallow a couple of bites while Jay kept the conversation going. He must have been lonely. He was a real talker. I heard the occasional word, while sitting still and erect as a soldier, waiting.

"I was born and raised in Washington, D.C., the third child in a family of seven kids. We lived on East Capitol Street and my wife-to-be lived just down the street. My family used to eat at the New England Raw Bar on Maine Avenue. Boy, that was a great place. My brother, Charlie, and me used to go to Griffith Stadium for baseball games. Of course, they knocked the thing down back in 1965, I think. We went to Redskin games where you could walk up and buy a ticket. Women would come dressed in high heels and fancy hats. These days, the kids come in those bell-bottoms and dirty looking t-shirts. What a shame."

And then, right on cue, the couple arose from their table, their eyes locked in lusty attraction. I watched them leave, hand in hand. A busboy swiftly appeared, gathered up the dirty dishes and reset the table. Dishes rattled, conversation buzzed, and Jay bantered on.

I realized I'd been holding my breath. I let it out slowly, waiting, staring with cold speculation.

And then everything seemed to drop into slow motion. I shut my eyes for just a moment and when I opened them, there she was. There *I* was, the 26-year-old me, an apparition, a ghost from the past, and yet she was flesh and blood, alive and so very young. The shock overwhelmed me, and I made a little sound of surprise.

"Charlotte… Charlotte, is everything okay?" Jay asked.

CHAPTER 17

My younger self was thin, much thinner than I recalled, and she stood proudly erect, her chin lifted in confidence. Had I really been that confident? I saw lush lashes, a swirl of bronze on her cheeks, and soft pink lipstick. Her skin was flawless, nose a little sharp. The hair was styled in a pale-blonde asymmetrical bob with inward-facing ends. She wore a royal blue shapeless shift with a dropped waist and white cuffs and collar, with matching medium heels. I recalled that dress. I had felt it was stylish but still conservative enough for the NSA.

It was bizarre how the image of my younger self that I'd held in memory was so dissimilar from the woman before me. I wasn't as pretty as I'd believed; not unattractive for sure, but my cheekbones weren't as high, my lips were thin and my legs skinny. The hairstyle looked hideous and was all wrong for the narrow shape of my face.

She had entered with Angie, a shorter girl with good hips, a broad face and a serious manner. Angie had worked as a secretary for Ed Kazenas, a dour, intelligent man in his fifties, who often met with President Nixon or his National Security staff, briefing them on the latest intelligence regarding Vietnam.

As I watched them sit, lost in quiet conversation, I grew dizzy and disoriented. It was too much to take in, and I was so electrically charged that I began to shiver. I was on the edge of fainting when I felt Jay's hand seize my arm. His concerned voice brought me back.

"Charlotte... you're as white as a ghost. Should we leave?"

I huffed out the anxiety, my eyes blinking rapidly. I struggled to return to full consciousness, but I couldn't stop trembling. Cyrano had been right. I needed to rest. I had to rest. Every cell in my body was fighting to stay awake.

After that, I don't remember much of what happened. I was in the lobby of the Willard Hotel when I was able to shake the mist of confusion and exhaustion.

Jay and I were standing by the bank of golden elevators.

"I really think you should see a doctor, Charlotte. You don't look well."

I looked into his earnest face and saw a gentle sorrow. "I'm sorry I ruined your dinner, Jay."

"Don't worry about that. I'm very concerned about you, Charlotte."

I smiled, grateful. "How nice a man you are, Jay. Thank you for saying that."

"Do you want me to go up with you?"

"No, I'll be fine now. I'm going straight to bed and get a good night's sleep. In the morning, everything will be fine. I'll be right as rain."

Jay nodded, lingering, hands thrust in his pants pockets. "Do you still want me to drive you around? I'm happy to, you know."

"Yes, I do."

He smiled his pleasure. "Well, then, you just call me when you're ready and old Jay will shoot right over."

I held his gaze for a moment. "Thank you, Jay. I'm greatly in your debt."

That pleased him. "Don't you worry about a thing. You just get some sleep."

After a shower, I eased into my new nightgown, slipped under the cool sheets and stared into the darkness. I couldn't stop the flow of tears. Seeing my 26-year-old self in the flesh had opened the tombs and resurrected the old ghosts, the old guilts, the painful open wounds. Would I be able to convince her of who I was and why I came? Would she listen and believe?

I prayed to God that He would give me the strength to carry out my plan. I prayed like I had never prayed before that I would not die in the night and leave my family to perish a second time in that terrible fire, in that raging inferno.

CHAPTER 18

Morning came and seemed to strike me like a hammer. My head pounded, my mouth was thick with syrupy saliva, and my eyes fluttered open, straining to focus. I could swallow, and I could breathe, but whenever I tried to move anything but my eyes, I couldn't. I panicked, mentally willing myself to move, but nothing happened. I couldn't move my arms or my legs, and worse, I couldn't feel them. I was on my back, helpless, heart kicking in my chest. I felt like a cold, hard, marble statue. I wanted to scream—to shout for help—but I had no voice and couldn't move my lips. What had happened? Had I had a stroke? No, no, please no. Metallic terror kept rising in my mouth.

The phone rang, but I couldn't move to answer it. It rang several times, stopped, and then rang again, like an alarm, like a warning, like a cry for help. When it finally stopped, the room became loud with a ringing silence.

I lay there, swallowing, mind churning, as I struggled to form a plan. Don't panic, I kept repeating.

Relax. Breathe. Relax every muscle like Kim Stein taught you. She prepared you for this. They had all worked tirelessly to prepare me for every possible contingency.

Okay, I shouted inside my head, "Stop the racing thoughts and take stock of what you *can* do."

I could see, although my vision was blurred. I could hear—there was a faraway sound of a police siren.

Relax. Breathe. Calm the mind. Imagine a soothing beach house by the sea. Puffy, white clouds, a gentle breeze.

I waited and breathed and fought a towering fear. The minutes crawled by. From mental exhaustion, I finally fell back asleep.

When I awoke, my eyes startled open. I was still on my back, staring up at the ceiling. I moved a finger, a hand, and felt a triumphant rush of hope. Good. Good. I moved my left arm and then the right. My breath came fast. I wiggled my toes. Moved my right foot and then my left. Both legs moved, and I could feel them! Gently, slowly, as if I might break, I lifted up on elbows.

A crashing relief filled my heart, and I sat up, leaning back against the headboard.

Gradually, the hotel room came into focus and, remarkably, I soon came to realize that my vision was clear and sharp, sharper than it had been in years. Sunlight leaked in from under the cream-colored draperies, and I saw a bowl of fruit on the coffee table so clearly that it shimmered with extravagant color. Intrigued, I glanced around the room at the emerald colored couch and tanned pillows. They were rich in color and texture.

On the cream-colored walls, I focused on a seascape oil painting. The bright yellow sailboat with billowing sails leaned into the wind; the children at play on the beach in the foreground seemed animated, and a big golden sun was so vivid, it threatened to come alive. What had happened? Had I ever seen this well? I looked at the clock on the night table. It was after 2 p.m. But what day? How long had I been out?

I tossed back the blanket and gently swung my feet to the deep, royal blue carpet and wiggled my toes again. It felt so good to just wiggle my toes and to take deep, calming breaths. As I gingerly rose to my feet, a surge of energy coursed through my body like an electric charge. I felt vital, supple and strong. But what had happened?

On impulse, I moved to the nearest mirror, an oval wall mirror, and stared back at myself. The hairs on the back of my neck and on my arms stood up. Ripples of shivery wonder passed through my body. Was I imagining it, or did I look younger? I nosed in closer and narrowed my eyes.

The needle-thin lines around my mouth were gone. The crows-feet around my eyes had smoothed. My neck flab was reduced, and those once restless, turbulent eyes were calm, clear; my dull gray hair now had a gleam and luster. As if touching a new face, I ran a finger along my pink cheeks, my skin now a creamy, healthy hue.

I stumbled back, found the nearest chair and dropped down into it, my mind spinning in disbelief. Minutes later I heaved myself out of the chair and back to the mirror to verify the change. It was true, I did look younger—maybe 10 or 15 years younger!

How could it be that I had gone from one extreme to the other—being completely incapacitated one hour, and energetic and younger the next?

None of the TEMPUS team had prepared me for this. Most thought the aging process would speed up, a result of the strenuous and arduous time travel, which is why Kim worked so hard strengthening my heart, mind and body.

Kim's words echoed back. "In all honesty, Charlotte, we have no idea what you are about to face. It's all new to us, as it will be to you."

I called the front desk and calmly asked what the time and day were.

The tentative female voice said, "It's 2:20 p.m., Friday May 31st."

I hung up and did a little dance. Had I ever done a little dance? I felt like Ebenezer Scrooge on Christmas Day, a changed and joyous human, after his dramatic encounter with the three spirits.

I paced to the windows and flung open the drapes. Sun streamed in. Gorgeous warm, welcoming sun. I gazed up into a lovely blue sky and took in another life-affirming breath. It was so good to be alive.

I dressed hurriedly, and instead of eating at the hotel, I decided to stroll, purse swinging, until I found a quaint restaurant or coffee shop that suited me. The hotel was located only two blocks away from the White House, so I ambled by, noticing how changed the surrounding area was from 2018. There were no barriers or extra security. It had a much more open feel to it, more welcoming and statelier. I decided to bypass the museums and memorials but roamed through the National Mall, recalling the 1963 March on Washington and Martin Luther King's *"I Have a Dream"* speech.

Paul and I had brought the kids to the Mall many times and Lacey loved to point up to the Washington Monument and say "Can I live up there some day? With George Washington?"

I was feeling a gaiety and optimism I hadn't felt in years. I felt right at home, returned to this simpler time before cell phones, emails, texts and the 24-hour news cycle. There were only three TV stations in 1968: NBC, CBS and ABC; no *YouTube*, cable or streaming. I delighted in viewing the cars, classics in 2018: Mustangs, Cameros, a Ford Galaxie, an impressive red Pontiac Bonneville, and an unexpected shiny 1967 blue Le Mans, the same model I had driven. Just seeing that car gave me a little lift.

The streets were bloated with anxious tourists and scattering children, their brochures and maps at the ready.

Young women strutted by, showing a sexy confidence I wasn't sure I'd ever possessed. I loved the fashion: the drainpipe jeans, the bell bottoms and Capri pants; the bright colors and funky tights; the miniskirts, the long hair and beards, the Afro hairdos and platform shoes.

Wafting from car radios and transistor radios was the music of Frank Sinatra, Marvin Gaye, Simon & Garfunkel and Jefferson Airplane.

I continued walking west, leaving the tourist areas, lost in a panorama of sight and memory, the warm, humid breeze and bright sun entrancing and life-affirming. This once-remembered past appeared more vibrant and real than I recalled or could have ever imagined. Had I sleepwalked through it the first time, hypnotized by commitment, duty and the endless details of intelligence gathering? Had I truly seen the world of 1968 for what it was and how it was unraveling?

When I saw an old glass phone booth, I stopped short, then moved on, with an uncertain stride. I stopped again and glanced back at it over my shoulder. It seemed to call to me. I squinted up into the hot sun, conflicted.

Inside the booth, I closed the folding door. I had the change, a dime. I lowered my gaze, nibbling on my lower lip, noticing a crumpled Butternut candy bar wrapper. Did they even make that candy anymore, in 2018?

I inserted the dime into the coin slot and listened to the "*Ding.*" I heard the dull droning of the dial tone.

Still unsure, I shut my eyes and massaged them, knowing full well I was going to call. I had to. Even though I'd seen my younger self the day before, I had to prove to myself that I had truly time traveled and that my family and that house were there. Using the rotary dial, I dialed the number I hadn't called in fifty years. It was time to contact the family I had come to save from certain death.

CHAPTER 19

"HELLO?"

It was Paul's voice. Paul, alive again. It was true. I had time traveled. Until now, I wasn't entirely certain. It could have been a hallucination or a dream. Maybe I had fallen into a coma before or after time traveling. But I heard Paul. It was Paul's smooth, baritone voice.

The shakes returned, and a thumping heart. My hand on the receiver shook so violently I nearly dropped the thing. I had no voice although I tried to speak. I tried to say his name, but I heard only a low whisper.

"Hello?" Paul repeated, more loudly. "Hello? Is anybody there?"

When I heard Lyn shout angrily in the background, "Daddy, Lacey took my candy!" I nearly fainted.

Paul hung up.

Once again, I stood on shaky legs, breath coming fast. I managed to yank open the heavy phone booth door and stumble outside into a gust of a breeze. A well-dressed man and woman passed, studying me with concern. Thankfully, they didn't stop.

I found a coffee shop nearby. I don't remember where I was or what the name was. I sat at the counter, on one of the eight round yellow swivel stools. Placed between a Heinz ketchup bottle and a glass sugar shaker sat a square tabletop jukebox, its gleaming chrome soft-lit by neon hues. It held my attention for a time while I recovered. I'd forgotten about those. You flipped through the jukebox menu, made a song selection, dropped 10 cents into the coin slot and pressed two buttons—one top letter and one bottom number. Seconds later, the song played.

Studying it was a good distraction while I waited for the coffee and tuna salad sandwich I had ordered. Behind the counter were soda spouts, an ice cream unit and a 1968 calendar with a poster of Elvis Presley, a strand of his gleaming raven hair falling carelessly over his forehead.

On the counter to my left was a vanilla cake, displayed under a large plastic cover. It caught my attention because Lyn loved vanilla cake. Lacey loved donuts. Next to the cake was a plate filled with sugar donuts. I felt the sting of tears as I reached for one, then stopped, feeling foolish, feeling a new bitterness. Why had God, or the fates put this cake and these stupid donuts in my face? Was it just a coincidence?

I averted my damp eyes and reached for the menu.

As I absently ate the sandwich, I grew aware of a woman seated next to me. She was about my age and was reading *The Washington Post.*

She made a tsk-tsk sound and shook her head. "It's shameful, all these student riots," she said, mostly to herself. "Just shameful. What do they hope to gain from all those sit-ins and flag burnings? Awful..."

And then she turned to me, her face all wadded up in irritation. She had lifeless steel gray hair, a doughy white face and sagging dark eyes.

"The world is going crazy. First, they killed President Kennedy, then Martin Luther King, and now everybody else is just going nuts."

"I beg your pardon?" I said.

The woman jabbed the paper with a finger. "Burning flags," she said with fresh disdain. "Those young good-for-nothing war protestors are burning flags."

Not wanting to get drawn into a conversation, I didn't engage. The woman was lost in her own world and didn't seem offended. She continued reading, making clucking sounds of outrage.

Outside, I rambled, my energy flagging, legs growing stiff. What was happening? Emotion and fear kept bullying me. If I can't even sustain a phone call, how am I ever going to meet my younger self face-to-face and explain who I am and why I came?

I could feel my energy rise and fall—spiking up one minute and dropping the next. Then my heart began to pound, and I was short of breath. Obviously, the time travel was playing havoc with my body.

Worried, I glanced about, desperate to spot a taxi. I didn't think I could make it back to the hotel on my own. Suddenly, the heat seemed stifling, and I gasped for breath. Just when I thought I couldn't take another step, I felt someone take my arm and hold me up.

Startled, I turned to look at the person. At first, my vision was cloudy, and I strained and blinked. I felt the strength of the man; felt his support. And then my eyes cleared, and his youthful, handsome face came into clear focus. I knew him. But it was impossible. I made a sharp cry of shock and fear as a coldness engulfed me.

It was Alex. Alex Mason from TEMPUS.

CHAPTER 20

I awoke in my hotel room. It was night. A light was on. I struggled awake and managed to push up enough to rest my back against the headboard. I gently wiped my eyes and, slowly, an image of Alex Mason appeared at the foot of my bed. I couldn't believe it. I kept blinking and staring, frightened, feeling very vulnerable.

"Hello, Charlotte," Alex said, with no smile, his expression rather solemn. He had the start of a beard and his hair seemed longer. Then I remembered that in the last month or so before I had time traveled, he'd started to let his hair grow.

"I don't understand," was all I could say.

He gave me a strange and vivid grin. "No, I don't suppose you do. It's a good thing I was following you. You'd be in the hospital now. Maybe even dead."

"Dead?"

"You were having a heart attack. I managed to get

you into a cab and back to the hotel. You were barely conscious when I got you here. I told the doorman you were my grandmother and that you had fainted from the heat. A couple of bellhops helped me get you to bed. I administered a shot to keep you alive, and another shot to help you relax and sleep. I'm surprised you're awake."

I shook my head in a slow wonder. "My head feels like it's stuffed with cotton. I'm so confused. I don't know where I am, or what world I'm living in, or even who I am. How did you get here?"

Alex adjusted his broad shoulders. He was dressed in tan khakis and a light blue polo shirt that revealed muscled arms and a wide chest.

I studied his face, a face I'd often felt seemed at war with itself.

"Tell me, Alex. What's going on?"

"How do you feel?"

"I've been better. Am I dying?"

"The shot should do the trick."

"My heart medication was ruined when I arrived. It was just a useless paste."

"I'll leave some medication. It's quite powerful. As they say, take as directed, just one tablet a day."

"And what is this drug?"

"The name? Elliptidine. It will never be marketed to the public."

"I'm not sure I like the sound of that."

"It will keep you alive."

"Why are you here, Alex, and how did you get here?"

He spread his hands. "Magic."

"Be serious. I need answers. Obviously, you all lied to me... Or maybe I haven't time traveled at all. Maybe this is all some clever drug-induced hallucination or a hologram. Tell me. Tell me now what this is all about."

He put his opened hand to the side of his temple and saluted. "Yes, ma'am. I'm a highly trained soldier. First and foremost, a soldier who also just happens to be a physicist."

I felt my left eye twitch. I was scared, and Alex must have seen it in my eyes.

"Don't look at me like that. I'm a good soldier who loves his country and wants the very best for it. Relax and don't be frightened. I'm not here to hurt you in any way."

I wasn't consoled. I waited for more.

Alex continued. "In many ways, you and I are a lot alike. You spent a lifetime sacrificing for your country. You believed in the country and I think you still do. You want the best for it and, if I may be altruistic and expansive, I think that you believe that if our country is better, and good and right, then the rest of the world will follow, and it will become better and good and right. Isn't that true, Charlotte?"

"I'm listening," I said.

Alex inhaled a little breath. He paced to the front windows and turned to look at me.

"You have indeed time traveled. This is Saturday, June 1, 1968, 3 a.m."

"Have you've been here since I collapsed? I mean since you brought me here?"

"I wanted to make sure you were okay. The shot I gave you is powerful and experimental. I didn't know if you'd make it. I want you to make it, Charlotte."

"Why?"

"So you can complete your mission."

"How did you get here? Why are you here, Alex?"

Slowly, reluctantly, he moved toward me. He shoved the gray tufted armchair to the side of my bed and eased down, folding his hands in his lap.

"I have a mission too."

I took in little breaths to stay calm.

"I got here by piggy-backing on top of you, so to speak. I could give you a technical explanation for it, but since you wouldn't understand, I won't."

"Have you done this before?" I asked.

From the ample lamplight, I saw Alex's eyes drop and then come back up. "We tried."

"And?"

"This is our first success. Charlotte, you are our first success."

"How many times have you tried?"

"Three."

"What happened to the other three?"

"Truth?"

I jerked a nod, summoning courage.

"They died."

There was a glass of water on the night table. I reached, drank half of it and then wriggled my upper body to sit more erect. Alex must have noticed my despondency.

"They all volunteered, Charlotte, just as you did.

They knew the risks."

"Were they all women?"

"One man, two women."

"Why did *I* make it… at least this far?"

"You had a mountain of guilt and an unhealthy dose of self-hatred. Once you saw the possibility of changing the past, you were able to transmute successfully those negative qualities into a positive, unshakeable intention. The others were killed by fear, doubt, a weak intention, or a flaw in our technology."

The room was so very quiet. I heard rain tapping the windows and had the bizarre feeling that Alex and I were the last people alive on Earth.

"Are you religious, Alex?"

The question caught him off guard. He slowly got up, keeping his questioning eyes on me.

"Not particularly. I assume you discussed your religious beliefs with Dr. Stein?"

"Yes… After my family died in the fire, all my childhood beliefs about a compassionate God died with them. Did you know my father was a Presbyterian minister?"

Alex lowered his head. "No, I didn't."

I stared down at my old, vein-ridden, wrinkled hands. "You said you had a mission. What is it?"

He moved to the side of my bed, lingered and smiled warmly. He reached and touched my arm with a gentleness that nearly brought tears. Except for Jay taking my arm in the deli, I hadn't been touched by a man—any man—in years.

"I bet you wonder how I knew where you were.

How I found you outside Gill's Coffee Shop?"

I didn't speak.

"You have a chip in the back of your neck. I have one too."

I felt my body heat up. "Then you were watching me?"

"Just for two days. I'm leaving tomorrow on a flight to Los Angeles."

"Your mission?" I asked.

He nodded. "Let's talk about the early morning of June 5, 1968."

Despite the little spasms of pain in my chest; despite the drugs, my reliable, sharp memory would never forget that day. I felt my eyes widen in recognition.

Alex folded his muscular arms. "Yes, Charlotte. That's my mission. It was another reason you were selected, bad heart and all. Your family died the same day that Bobby Kennedy was shot and killed. We know that 24-year-old Sirhan Bishara Sirhan shot Kennedy. I'm going to Los Angeles to make sure Bobby Kennedy is not killed. My mission is to kill Sirhan Sirhan and let Bobby Kennedy become the 37th President of the United States."

My body turned ice-cold.

CHAPTER 21

"I THINK YOU'LL get a kick out of this place, Charlotte," Jay said, as we drove along a two-lane asphalt road under glorious, early Saturday afternoon sunshine. We passed rolling fields, alive with colorful wildflowers and a grove of trees. In 2018, this land had been developed with rambling condos and three-story corporate offices, featuring manicured lawns and parking lots.

"We'll get some gas at a Sunoco Station, and then just across the street is a little beer joint on the left. It has a takeout window for beer and sandwiches, and there are some picnic benches. It's a lot of fun, and I haven't been out here in a couple of years."

I tried to appear enthusiastic, but my mind kept playing back bits and pieces of the conversation I'd had with Alex Mason at three o'clock that morning. My watch said it was 1:20 p.m. Alex was on board a 707, on his way to Los Angeles to complete "his mission."

"Don't worry," Jay said, "We'll work our way over to Marlow Heights, so you can take a look at the neighborhood."

Just hearing the name Marlow Heights unnerved me, but I knew I had to go. I had to shake off the emotional storms that kept overwhelming me. As Alex would say, I had to complete my mission. Time was running out.

Jay turned to me. "I know I keep saying it, but I'm glad you decided to come out with me. I was worried about you, Charlotte. When you didn't answer your phone, I began to imagine all kinds of things. I always did have a fertile imagination."

"It was good of you to check on me," I said, sincerely. "And it's generous of you to chauffeur me around like this."

"Generous? Charlotte, this is the most fun I've had in a long time. I haven't taken a leisurely drive in... well, I don't remember when. When I was a boy, after church and our Sunday meal, we would all pile into Dad's Model T Ford and drive all over the place. They were mostly dirt roads back in those days, of course, and when it rained, whoo-ee, was there mud. Well, on rainy Sundays I guess we didn't go far. Did you go for Sunday drives?"

I smiled reflectively. "Yes, sometimes. They were simpler times, weren't they, Jay?"

"Oh, my yes, they were. I just don't understand much of anything anymore in this country. All the riots and protests... all the anger. What has happened to us?"

I thought of Alex and the last talk we had before he left for the airport. We had already been talking for what seemed like hours, but it was still night, and rain still struck at the windows.

Alex hadn't shown any sign of fatigue. If anything, he seemed enlivened and enthusiastic.

I had managed to leave the bed, belt on a robe and sit on the couch across from him.

"Charlotte, I time traveled so I could change the past and make the future a better place."

"But there's no guarantee that after you kill Sirhan Sirhan, Bobby Kennedy will get elected president," I said, forcefully. "You've lived long enough to know there are no guarantees in life. Anything can happen. Even with our best intentions, things can go horribly wrong. I saw it happen many times while working for the NSA."

Alex appraised me soberly. "I studied every aspect of the 1960s and the possibility of Robert Kennedy becoming president. By the way, did you know that Bobby had to repeat the third grade?"

"No, I didn't."

Alex continued. "Well, okay, it is far from a sure bet that RFK would have been nominated, and if nominated, elected. But he was winning most of the primaries at the time and under the old rules of that time, as you know, Charlotte, the bosses still controlled the Democratic Party. Hubert Humphrey, LBJ's vice president, was the favorite of the bosses. Kennedy was regarded as too radical, but he was counting on Chicago

Mayor Richard Daley to help him. And, yes, RFK would face a tough adversary in Richard Nixon in November, but he would have helped lead the United States into a more enlightened era."

I said, "But Nixon was building a silent majority of white middle-class Americans, scared to death of rioting blacks and the hippie college radicals. I recall it all very well, Alex. I lived in those days and I read the newspapers and saw the intelligence every day. That's why I worked so many hours. I thought I was helping to save the country, and maybe even the world. I, like many in those days, was committed to saving this country, no matter what it took."

Alex nodded. "Yes, you were, and it wasn't your fault that some senseless random fire killed your family. I read the report. The fire inspector said it was most likely caused by an overloaded electrical outlet or extension cord. Electrical fires travel fast. The smoke probably killed your family before the fire."

I shut my eyes, shaking my head. "I know all this," I snapped. "I don't need to hear it again."

"I'm sorry, Charlotte…"

I opened my eyes, sudden anger rising. "Alex, what you're about to do is too risky and immoral. You are going to rupture history. Who knows what chaos could come from it?"

Alex laughed, but it was a dark laugh. "Look at the chaos we were experiencing every day back in 2018. Look at what's going on in this city now in 1968. Flower children protesting; students burning draft cards. A pointless war killing thousands of young men. Good men, who are being wasted in those rice patties. I've got to try this."

"You can't change history, Alex. It's already happened."

"Charlotte, use your smart head. We're both here. We've already changed it. If you save your family, you will have changed history big time. I'll do the same with my mission. That's why we both came here, remember?"

I looked away, sighing audibly.

Alex softened his voice. "Look, Bobby Kennedy was riding a wave of change, struggling to put together a coalition of haves and have-nots. They were working tirelessly to end the war in Vietnam, which we know now was an absolute disaster for the United States. RFK was also tackling the problems of race and poverty."

I held up a hand. "Alex, had RFK survived and won the presidency, he would have found it nearly impossible to get us out of Vietnam. And withdrawing a half million men from Vietnam would have taken at least a couple of years. Also, regarding poverty, he would have run head-on into organized labor, and they were powerful in those days. Big labor did not want to create low-paying jobs for unskilled workers. That would have threatened the powerful unions. Alex, all I'm saying is that your mission may not produce the results you're hoping for. Killing Sirhan Sirhan may not fix anything at all, but only make things worse. Anyway, Nixon will most surely be elected, not Bobby Kennedy. You're taking a big chance."

Alex pushed up, glaring down at me with an inflammatory face. "I didn't come all this way on a chance, Charlotte. I don't just intend to kill Sirhan Sirhan. I also plan to kill Richard Nixon."

He must have seen that my face was blank with shock.

Alex closed the distance between us and leaned in close. "Yes, Charlotte. Not chance. Action. Don't you remember the paranoia that pervaded the White House during the administrations of Johnson and Nixon, as public discontent over the Vietnam War grew? Think about how it poisoned everything and everyone. I'm sure you were in the thick of it at the NSA."

The hair at my neck was damp and sticky. I licked my dry lips but couldn't find any words.

Alex grinned with satisfaction. "Think of it, Charlotte. The Vietnam War will come to an end; the riots will end; there will be no Watergate scandal, and the country will be spared Nixon's corruption and the humiliation of his resignation. In other words, those turbulent times, which set the stage for our own turbulent times, will have never happened."

I stared ahead into unknown distances, pulsing with anxiety.

Alex squared his shoulders. "You see, it's not really about politics. No, not really; whether you're a Republican or a Democrat. It's about saving the country from itself. I'm sure you remember Eugene McCarthy. He was also campaigning to become the Democratic candidate. I spent hours memorizing his speeches. In one of his best he said,

> 'I run because this country is now in
> volved in a deep crisis of leadership;
> a crisis of national purpose—and a cri
> sis of American ideals. It is time to
> substitute a leadership of hope for a
> leadership of fear. This is not simply
> what I want, or what most of us want.
> It is, I believe, the deepest hunger of
> the American soul.'"

I stared coldly at Alex, seeing a sharp, predatory face, and it scared the hell out of me.

Alex continued. "So you see, Charlotte, it's about saving the country from its worst instincts. I time traveled so I could help make the world a better place, and that's exactly what I intend to do."

CHAPTER 22

The knot of fear in my gut didn't diminish after Alex left my hotel room for the airport. I tossed and turned until mid-morning, finally forcing myself up, calling room service and ordering a light breakfast. While I ate a corn muffin and sipped black coffee, I used the hotel stationary to jot down some ideas.

Should I contact some of my old colleagues at the NSA and tell them of Alex's plans? But how could I? A security check of my alias, Charlotte Wilson, would reveal I had no past or present. Charlotte Wilson was a nobody in this time, and my passport would quickly be exposed as a fake. If they somehow tracked me down, they'd lock me up, and I wouldn't be able to complete my mission: saving my family.

But I had to do something. The people at TEMPUS had lied to me and used me. If they had told me the true reason I'd been selected, would I still have agreed to time travel? I don't know. Still, my moral and ethical compass propelled me to act—I had to try to tell someone.

About an hour later, I decided to contact two colleagues at the NSA anonymously, Kent Reed and Ed Kazenas. I would send them a letter through priority channels, knowing they'd receive it swiftly. Even though we received many such "crazy" letters frequently, as did the CIA and FBI, I had to try to get through. If I worded the letter just right, perhaps if I included specific facts and closed with secret information they would recognize, maybe, just maybe, they would act. Maybe they would contact the FBI, CIA, LAPD and Secret Service, and stop Alex from killing Sirhan and Richard Nixon.

I purchased stationery and a pen from the gift shop and finished the letter to my colleagues an hour later. I then wrote a short letter to young Charlotte, adding events about her life that only she and I would know. After reading it, I was certain she'd meet me, demanding answers. I would deliver young Charlotte's letter in person, when the family was away from the house.

I would have to find a way to have the letter delivered to the NSA, and I didn't want the letter traceable to me.

I dressed modestly, grabbed a broad-brimmed hat and sunglasses, and left the hotel.

I caught a cab and traveled to 16th Street NW to the Hay-Adams Hotel. If anyone tried to locate the sender of my letter to the NSA, and if they identified the bellhop, they'd start their search at the Hay-Adams, not the Willard.

Once inside, I found a courteous and ready bellhop. I handed him the sealed priority letter and a twenty-dollar bill. I kindly asked him to have it sent via messenger to the NSA. I told him it was for my daughter who worked there.

He grew nervous and doubtful until I handed him another twenty. His smile and bow were reassuring. Would he have the letter delivered, or would he pocket the money and toss the thing aside? I had to hope that the letter would be sent and received.

Back at the hotel, I dozed for an hour before I was awakened by Jay's phone call. He was downstairs, waiting to go for a drive.

In Jay's car, I had difficulty stilling my jumpy thoughts and focusing on where I was.

Jay glanced over. "Are you still with me, Charlotte? You seem a hundred miles away."

I snapped back to the present, managing a strained smile.

"I'm sorry… I'm fine. I just didn't sleep very well last night."

Jay smiled broadly, removing a hand from the steering wheel, indicating toward the day. "If you want, I can pull over and you can take a little cat nap."

"No, no, Jay. I'm okay. Really."

"I want you to enjoy yourself. Here we are out on a beautiful sunny day, having ourselves a great time. Oh look, there's the Sunoco station."

After Jay and I finished our sandwiches and beer, we drove to Marlow Heights, my old neighborhood. I felt butterflies in my stomach as I directed Jay to Temple Hill Road, had him turn right on Leslie Avenue and then drive slowly along the tree-lined street until we came to 2407. The 1960s era had brought an influx of split-level homes and brick Ramblers. Our house was neither. And when I saw it, I nearly cried out in joy.

There it was. Our historic two-story turn-of-the-century house was there. The graceful white porch with a swing was there, where Lacey and Lyn had swung, kicking their feet, laughing. The four bedrooms, three baths were still there. The two sets of pocket doors, open staircase and back staircase were there. The walk-in bays, the original kitchen pantry, the wood floors, the gingerbread accents on the exterior, all there.

Jay pulled to the curb while I stared, overcome with emotion. I knew the family was at the Marlow Heights Shopping Center, enjoying the carnivals they ran every summer.

I left the car with tears swimming in my eyes. I walked purposefully down that front walkway, climbed the four concrete stairs to the porch and slipped the letter I'd written to young Charlotte under the front door.

Would the note convince her to meet me? I could only hope. I asked her to meet me the next day, Sunday, at 7 p.m. at Duke Zeibert's Restaurant, just off Connecticut Avenue.

After we drove away, Jay was aware of my emotional state.

He said, softly. "Would you like to go to the free concert at The Watergate? It might be pleasant to sit along the banks of the Potomac River."

I stared ahead, praying that young Charlotte would show up.

"Yes, Jay. I think that would be very nice. I had forgotten about those concerts."

CHAPTER 23

Duke Zeibert's Restaurant was long gone in 2018, but in the 1960s, I had often met friends from work there. It was decorated in wood and open brick, with white tablecloths, a rustic wagon wheel chandelier and soft blue carpet. Large caricatures of the owner engaged in various sports hung on the walls. For many years, it was *the* place for politicians and businessmen to meet for power lunches. It would be a little more subdued on a Sunday during dinner.

When I'd made the reservation, I'd asked to be seated at a table near the mahogany bar, knowing that the noise level would be high, thereby masking our conversation.

I arrived early, at 6:45, and was seated with a menu. I slipped on my reading glasses and was all nerves and moving hands. I had only to glance at the menu to recall what the place was known for: Duke's Delights:

Boiled Beef in Pot, Boiled Chicken in Pot, Maine Lobster and thick-cut Prime Rib of Beef.

At 7 p.m., I ordered a daiquiri, in memory of the old days. It was only 50 cents, and the entrees averaged six dollars.

At ten minutes after seven, I sipped the daiquiri, hoping the rum would help to soothe a mounting disappointment. At 7:15, the noise level swelled, and the friendly waiter drifted over to ask if I'd like to order. I said I'd wait. I ordered another daiquiri.

At 7:22, I saw her. In my note, I'd described my physical appearance and told her where I'd be sitting. She nervously searched the room and, when she found me, her face expressed an anxious tension. I'm sure mine did too. I sat frozen in my chair.

The print dress she wore had short sleeves and cheerful yellow and blue stripes. I recalled that I had purchased it at Lansburgh Department Store, and it wasn't as comfortable as it had been in the fitting room. I easily remembered the store was on the 400 block of 7th Street, N.W. in the shopping district. It had closed in 1973.

But what I had forgotten were those shoes. They were navy blue with small square heels and a single Mary Jane strap, just like a doll's shoes.

Young Charlotte's upturned nose, fine neck and hair-sprayed modified beehive all gave her a convincing elegance. Men at the bar noticed her and swiveled around on their bar stools to gawk. I didn't recall drawing that much male attention, but then I was always living in my head, wasn't I? A head packed full of a hodgepodge of languages and data that I was constantly shifting around and trying to interpret.

She approached, and I hardly breathed, as if expecting an attack. The young, toothy hostess indicated toward the chair opposite me, but young Charlotte ignored her and remained standing. Finally, the hostess gave a little shrug, dropped the menu at the place-setting and moved away.

My young self stared at me, not with a small amount of malice. "Who are you?"

I found my voice. "Please sit down."

"Not until you tell me who you are and what you're after."

Men still had their interested eyes on her.

"Do you want to make a scene, Mrs. Vance?" I asked, looking about. Three people at the next table were looking on curiously.

I knew that the younger me was private and did not like attention. She lowered herself in the chair but kept her burning eyes on me.

"Would you like a drink?" I said, fighting for calm.

There are no words to describe the absolute terror that struck as I stared at a living, breathing image of myself from another time. I felt an astonished agony. I wanted to cry, laugh and run away. I wanted to blurt out all the wisdom I had learned the hard way. I wanted to express the regrets and bare my soul, as I felt my time was running out and my death was inching ever closer. I wanted to say that unless you listen to everything I say, and believe it, and take it to heart and act on it, you will feel like the lowest person on this planet and hate yourself for the rest of your life.

She projected an impression of strength, but I knew she was shaken.

The waiter appeared, and she brushed him away, her hard eyes locked on me.

She lowered her voice, just enough so that I could hear. "What do you want?"

I coolly took sips from my cocktail, waiting for her to calm down.

"I'm a friend," I finally said.

Her eyes enlarged. "A friend of whom? What? How did you know those things about me? Nobody knows those things you wrote about me in your letter," she said, in a harsh whisper, as she glanced about self-consciously. "Nobody. Those were private and personal things. How did you know I burned my diary back in 1961? Who have you been talking to?"

I tried to give her an honest expression. "I wrote those things in the letter so that you would meet me. I'm not out to hurt you or your family in any way."

She narrowed her suspicious eyes on me, and when she spoke, her voice trembled. She was obviously frightened. "Who are you working for? Which agency?"

I shook my head. "I don't work for any agency. Mrs. Vance, all I'm asking is that you relax and listen to what I have to say."

She sat back dismissively, crossing her arms tightly across her chest. Her eyes slid away from any direct glance. "So talk. I'm listening. And make it fast. I don't have much time."

"You don't have time because you're always going to the office, aren't you? You're rarely home for dinner with your family, and they miss you. No, Mrs. Vance, you work till 10 or 11 p.m. and then drive home, still preoccupied with the details of your job. You kiss Lyn and Lacey, pull the sheet up to Lacey's chin, because she always kicks the sheet off. She has bad dreams, you know. She awakens at least twice a week, screaming. Paul goes in to comfort her. Most of the time, you're not home yet. You're working. Paul tells you about Lacey's bad dreams, but often you're preoccupied with, oh, let's say, *Minaret*."

Young Charlotte jerked erect, shooting me a startled glance. She leaned in toward me, her face suddenly flushed with alarm.

"What are you saying? How do you know about…" She lowered her voice even more. "How do you know about *Minaret*? That is top secret."

I nodded. "Have I got your attention, Mrs. Vance?"

She sat as still as a statue, and I could almost hear her mind working.

I continued. "Who decided to task the NSA with monitoring certain communications to high level government officials, Mrs. Vance? The simple fact is that the NSA is now secretly intercepting the telephone calls and telegrams of at least two U.S. senators, at the White House's request. I won't mention names."

Young Charlotte's face kept changing expressions: shock, concern, confusion. Her face twisted and went vacant. Slowly, it cleared, and her voice took on a threatening edge.

"I'll have you arrested and thrown into prison," she said, through clinched teeth.

I wondered if I had gone too far. "Mrs. Vance... My point is, your family should come first. You should go home tonight and be with your family. Work will always be there. Work can wait. Kids can't wait. They grow up fast and if you're not there, you'll miss one of the most important parts of your life, and when you get to my age, you'll have a mountain of regrets and so much pain that you can barely get on with your day."

Young Charlotte's eyes changed. Her voice was hesitant and low, and it held fear. "Who are you? How do you know all these... secrets?"

I gave her a sweet and sad smile. "Please listen to me, Mrs. Vance. Please listen very closely. On June 4th, don't go to work. Take your husband and children on a trip. Take them anywhere. Go visit your father in Vermont. Go visit your best friend in college. She lives in Virginia Beach. You've always loved Ocean Beach. Go to Ocean Beach, or any beach. Whatever you do, take your family and leave town before the night of June 4th. Please listen to me and do this, Mrs. Vance."

I saw a new blaze of fear rise in her eyes. She shot up and the force of her anger was palpable.

"If you ever try to see me or my family again; if you ever call me again; if I ever hear from you again, I will have you arrested and locked away. Do you understand me?"

I looked up into her eyes and tried to convey warmth. "I don't care what happens to me, Mrs.

Vance. Please just do as I say."

In that searing moment, our eyes truly met. Her eyes deepened and probed mine, as if she were peering into a dark room, searching for light. Suddenly, she stumbled backwards, grabbing the back of a chair to brace herself.

Had she recognized herself in me? I nearly pushed to my feet but paused, hope building.

She leaned in close with wild, staring eyes. "You are completely out of your mind," she said, venomously. "Don't ever contact me again."

She pivoted and marched out of the restaurant, swinging her purse over her shoulder, many eyes following her as she left the restaurant. I sat listless and depressed. But I wasn't finished with her yet. I'd already set my back-up plan in motion. The letter I'd sent to the NSA might wake her up. All I could do was hope that she'd put two and two together and take the necessary action to save her family.

But she might not. So as a final plan, I decided I would have to go to the house and somehow get my family out. Young Charlotte probably wouldn't be there. I would call Paul and warn him, but if he didn't believe me, then I would wait until just before that terrible hour and I would call the fire department. I'd hammer on the front door, break a window or do whatever I had to do to get them out of that house before the blazing fire collapsed the roof. I would get them out of that house any way I could, as long as my heart kept me alive.

CHAPTER 24

I'd blown it, but then I knew I would. I had never been good at diplomacy or negotiation. Paul was skilled at both, but then Paul was skilled at most things. Paul was definitely the better half of our marriage, and I say that not in self-pity, but in all honesty.

Sunday night, after I left Duke Zeibert's Restaurant, I walked the streets in an awful expectation. I couldn't still my agitated mind or my emotions. After a quick drink at the hotel bar, I returned to my room, took a shower, swallowed one of Alex's blue heart pills, and sat down at the little writing desk. I decided that it was time to write down everything that had happened to me in a clear, logical order, beginning with my initial meeting with Luke Baker, when I first learned about TEMPUS.

I needed to ensure that young Charlotte would have a true and accurate account of all the facts. I wanted her to know who I was, and why I'd time traveled. I wanted TEMPUS to be held responsible for everything that was about to happen and, in an accompanying letter, I would plead with young Charlotte to save this account. I would request that she return to TEMPUS in fifty years, in 2018, and personally hand deliver my account to Cyrano Conklin. I wanted him to know that I had finally realized what they had been up to: that they had used me to transport Alex for their own devious and unscrupulous ends.

Of course, I had no control over what my younger self would do with the account. Since I had already nudged the future in a different direction by meeting with her, I didn't know how she would respond. Would she keep the account, turn it over to Steven Case, her boss, or would she burn it, believing that I was, in fact, out of my mind? Since I wasn't even able to convince her of the urgency to leave town, I could only hope that after everything unfolded, she would eventually believe me and see that my written account was handed to Cyrano in 2018.

I wrote swiftly, until my hand cramped and my eyes grew sandy; until I glanced over at the clock to see it was after three in the morning.

I came bursting out of sleep at 8:30 the following day. It was already June 3rd. I went shuffling to the bathroom to swallow another blue heart pill. I didn't feel well, but oddly, I was hungry. I ordered breakfast from room service, and while I ate, I returned to the writing desk. As I wrote, I realized I had to do something with the $40,000 in cash I still had with me. I dressed quickly and went to a nearby bank to open a safe deposit box.

I returned to the hotel and wrote furiously until after four. I was nearly finished, so I laid down on the bed for a few minutes of much-needed rest when the telephone rang.

"Charlotte, it's Jay. Did I wake you? You sound sleepy."

I sat up and tried to stifle a yawn. "I'm fine. I was just resting."

"I know it's late, but if you don't have other plans, I was wondering if you'd like to come over tonight and watch a movie with me. There's a great Western on Channel 4 at nine o'clock. You remember you said you'd watch a Western with me?"

I smiled. "Yes, Jay, I remember."

"Have you ever seen *Shane*?"

"I don't think so. I may have, but I don't remember."

"You'll love it. I saw it in the movie theatre back in 1953 or 1954, I think it was. It has a great cast: Alan Ladd and Jean Arthur. Dinner is on me."

"How can I resist that?" I said.

"I make the best TV dinners in town. The trick is not to overcook them and to add a little side of cranberry sauce. Then it always feels a little like Thanksgiving dinner."

I laughed, and it felt good to laugh. Somehow, Jay could make me laugh when I didn't feel like it.

"Chicken, Turkey or Beef?" Jay asked.

"Turkey will be fine."

"I also have beer. That okay?"

"Good."

"Okay then. I'll come by and pick you up in a half hour."

Jay's house was a simple two-story, with a gabled roof and dormers; a little front lawn, trimmed hedges and a porch where metal chairs, with white and yellow armrests, made it feel homey.

Inside, the rooms were spacious, with a tan wall-to-wall shag carpet in the living room and avocado colored couch and chairs. The dining room was a woman's room, with wood floors and lace doily place mats on the polished oak table. Corner cabinets displayed the fine dishes, and on the walls were clumsy and unfortunate wood framed paintings of flowers and seascapes.

Jay pointed at the paintings, somewhat proudly. "Sally Ann painted them. I used to love watching her paint. She'd get the paint all over herself. I think they're rather good, don't you?"

I nodded, touched by his tenderness for them. "Yes. Nice."

He faced the room. "I only use this room now when the kids come for Thanksgiving and Christmas. I left it just as Sally Ann left it the day she died. Call me sentimental."

To my surprise, we settled in Jay's den, a comfortable room of wood floors, a swallow-you-up brown couch and a recliner near the emerald fireplace and two cherry wood bookshelves filled with books. The TV, with rabbit ears, stood in the far corner.

"What a lovely room," I said. "Obviously, you're a reader."

Jay pocketed his hands and rocked on his heels as he took in his collection of hardbacks and paperbacks.

"Yes, I do like to read—detective stories, mostly. And some history. I did well in history in school."

I noticed the blue shirt he wore heightened his silver-gray hair and deep blue eyes. I hadn't really studied Jay all that much. I'd been so preoccupied with other things. He had a good face, not especially handsome, but a kind, friendly face and warm eyes. If his nose was a bit big, he had a good jaw, good shoulders and just a little tummy. It was his smile I liked most. It was an honest, joyful smile that seem to say, *I like living. I'm comfortable living in my own skin*.

We rested our TV dinners on TV stands, munching the dinners while acutely engaged in the color movie that Jay said was filmed on location in Jackson Hole, Wyoming. For a time, I forgot my life, and all the difficulties, and what was to come.

As the movie unfolded, Shane made several attempts to put his gun fighting days behind him. But he was forced to draw his guns and kill, to protect his adopted family.

I glanced over at Jay, whose eyes were glued to the TV screen like a kid. Shane had been wounded in the gunfight, and Jay knew what was to come, having seen the movie at least three times.

Tears rolled down Jay's cheeks as Shane mounted his horse and rode away. Joey (the young boy who looks up to him) keeps calling after him "Shane! Come back, Shane!"

When THE END rolled across the screen, Jay pushed up, abruptly, and left for the bathroom.

Minutes later, he returned with two more beers. He popped the tab and handed one to me. "That is one helluva movie, isn't it?" he asked.

I took a swallow of the beer. "I don't understand why he rode off like that. Why didn't he stay? Is he leaving because he doesn't want to die in front of Joey?"

Jay eased back down in his chair, set his beer on the stand, and made a tent of his fingers. "Yes, and also because there's no place left for him anymore in the changing world. His life, as he knew it as a gunfighter in the old West, is over."

I didn't want to think about that too hard. I had returned to a world I'd already lived in, and its culture, technology and character were now somewhat alien to me, and in stark contrast to the one I'd come from in 2018. Assuming I'd be able to prevent the fire from killing my family, I had the feeling that I would want to mount my horse, so to speak, and ride off into the sunset like Shane.

After bowls of chocolate ice cream and cups of coffee, I stood and reached for Jay's bowl.

"I'll clean up," I said.

Jay stopped me. He rose and reached for my wrist, holding it gently. He lowered his earnest eyes and took me in.

"I've got something I want to say, Charlotte, and I don't want you to say anything until after I've finished. Just listen and think about it."

I steadied myself with an effort. There was a sharp gleam of hope in his eyes, and I knew what he was going to say. I wanted to turn and go, but I couldn't hurt Jay's feelings. He was a good and sensitive man, so I listened, avoiding his eyes.

CHAPTER 25

I waited as Jay screwed up the courage to speak.
He indicated toward the room. "Charlotte… this is nice, isn't it? I mean, how we sat here tonight, and talked, laughed, ate TV dinners and watched a movie. It was a good thing, wasn't it?"

I ducked my head, stooped and picked up his bowl, stacked it in mine and took a step back, so he had to release my wrist. "Yes, Jay. I had a lot of fun."

Jay swallowed, shoved his hands into his pockets and stood awkwardly. "I like you, Charlotte. I liked you from the first. You're good people. You're fun. You're smart, and you're a very attractive woman."

I shut my eyes, shaking my head. "I'm *not* attractive, Jay. I'm an old woman who's had her day and could die at any minute."

"Don't say that. You shouldn't say that about yourself—or about your life. None of us knows how much time we've got left here on this good Earth. Only God knows that. What we should do is live our life the best we can, for as long as we can. Don't you think so?"

I couldn't face him. "I don't know. I haven't had time to think about…"

Jay cut me off. "… We have fun together, don't we? I mean, right from the start we had fun. We laugh at the same things. Okay, I guess what I'm saying, and not very well, because I haven't felt this way in a real long time but… Charlotte, I'd like us to be together. I mean, not just as friends. I'm sixty-eight years old, and I've been lonely for a long time. I'm not the loner type. I was married to Sally Ann for forty-six years., and I liked being married. I was faithful to her every day of my life. Now, I'm not saying we need to jump right into marriage or anything. We'll wait some weeks or months and just see how things go."

I couldn't believe what I was hearing. It jarred me. I liked Jay, but I just couldn't think about any other thing until I stopped that damned fire from killing my family. That's why I had come. What happens later? I had no idea.

We stood in a gathering silence. I heard a dog bark outside. I heard the roar of a car engine starting next door.

I looked into Jay's hopeful eyes. "Jay… I'm seventy-six years old."

"No, you're not."

"I am."

"Well, you look sixty… even younger."

"You're a sweet man, Jay. I like you very much. Ask me again in a few days. Ask me next weekend."

I gave him a warm smile and hoped he didn't notice my lying eyes. I didn't intend to be in Washington in a week.

"Thank you, Jay. Thank you for a wonderful evening… and you were right about the cranberry sauce. It did seem a lot like Thanksgiving dinner."

Jay took a step toward me, leaned and kissed me softly on the lips.

"You're a fine woman, Charlotte. Don't ever believe otherwise. And you can bet that I will ask you again this weekend. How does Friday night sound?"

"I was thinking about a date early Wednesday morning," I said softly. I was relieved when he smiled and nodded, without asking questions.

The final chance to save my family would take place before dawn on Wednesday morning, June 5, 1968, and I knew now that Jay would be the one to help me carry out my plans.

Thus, ends my true and accurate account of all events that have occurred since my first meeting with Luke Baker, in February 2018. It is my sincere wish that this account be delivered to Cyrano Conklin of TEMPUS, by Charlotte Vance, in 2018.

Charlotte Wilson
Washington, DC
June 3, 1968

PART 3

CHAPTER 26

Monday evening, June 3rd, 26-year-old Charlotte was working late at the NSA. She sat stiffly in her office chair, a cigarette going in the ashtray, a pile of folders on her desk and two accordion files on the floor to her right. Before her lay type-written memos, correspondence and highlighted hand-written notes on a legal pad. All the data before her concerned *Minaret*, a top-secret project that few people knew anything about.

She was distracted and nervous, working hard to stop her mind from racing, from thinking about that old woman in Duke Zeibert's Restaurant the previous night. She wanted to erase the emotions that meeting had stirred up.

Charlotte stood and reached for her cigarette, moving toward the windows. She inhaled and blew a cloud of smoke, looking down at the NSA parking lot. Only that morning, Lacey had said, "Mommy, Daddy said you work in a big, glass fairy castle. Do you work with fairies, Mommy?"

Charlotte smiled at the memory and then returned to her chair, lowering her eyes on a memo she'd received that morning from her boss, Steven Case. She scanned it quickly, her head crowded with thoughts.

```
NSA Launches 'Canyon' Surveillance
Satellites

The NSA launched the first of seven
satellites, code named "Canyon," that
can pick up various types of voice and
data traffic from Earth's orbit. Canyon
will lead to a more sophisticated sat
ellite intelligence system, code named
"Rhyolite."
```

Charlotte leaned back, smoking and thinking. How could that old woman have known about *Minaret*? Did she also know about *Rhyolite*? Was she a spy? For whom?

Equally disturbing, how could she have possibly known about Tommy Webber, the first boy she'd had sex with? Nobody, even Paul, knew about that. She'd always been too ashamed of that incident to tell anyone, including her best girlfriend.

Tommy had been a lowlife—a bad boy whom all the girls knew was no good, but as young and silly girls often do, they found him sexy. He was two years older than she and he rode a motorcycle, had long, sweptback greasy hair, and wore a black leather jacket. Okay, maybe he reminded her a little of Marlon Brando in the movie *The Wild Ones*. She did allow herself that one rationalization.

As usual, the imagination of sex with him was far superior to the reality. He smelled, he was forceful and quick, and he was stupid. No, she'd been stupid for going out with him. She'd been a mindless, love-crazed girl of seventeen, who wanted to rebel and shock her strict and cold father, not that she ever had the courage to tell him. She'd never told anyone about that disgusting night, and she'd never had sex with Tommy Webber again. The last she'd heard, he'd been killed in Vietnam.

So how did the old woman know? And how did she know about the ceremonial burning of that diary in 1961? There was no possible, logical answer, except that she was working with someone else and they were plotting extortion. But with whom?

Charlotte crushed out her cigarette and pushed up, wrapping herself with her arms. She was suddenly chilled. It was that woman's eyes that spooked her; those old eyes that held truth and a weary wisdom. When Charlotte gazed deeply into them, she felt an electric shock. They were familiar and pleading. For just a second, Charlotte saw something, sensed something. There was a second of some ineffable recognition, and yet she had never met this woman before.

Charlotte paced the room for a time and then slouched back down in her chair and reached for her paper cup of cold coffee. Absently, she took a sip. Why hadn't she asked for the woman's name and address? Simple. The old woman scared the hell out of her.

Charlotte slid her hesitant eyes toward the wall calendar. It was Monday, June 3rd, and it was 6:30 p.m. The old lady had suggested that Charlotte take June 4th off and leave town with her family. It was preposterous. And yet, there was something about the woman—something about her old, forceful eyes that was unnerving.

Minutes later, Steven Case entered, a pipe in one hand, a single-typed page in the other, his face filled with concern. He closed the door softly behind him and stood still, staring at her and then beyond her. She'd grown used to that. He always seemed to be living in another world.

Finally, he sat down, taking a couple of thoughtful puffs on his pipe. Under the artificial light, his brush-cut, steel-gray hair made him look severe. His white shirt was still crisp after a long day, the dark tie perfectly knotted at the neck, and his slacks still holding a crease.

"Charlotte, Kent Reed and Ed Kazenas just left my office. It seems that late Saturday evening they received a priority correspondence from the outside. It concerns a 24-year-old man named Sirhan Bishara Sirhan, who the letter claims may shoot and kill Bobby Kennedy. They spent most of Sunday, examining the letter and its contents before bringing it to my attention."

Charlotte leaned forward, folding her hands on the desk. The information was not especially unusual; some nut was always threatening to shoot some politician.

Steven went on. "Now, interestingly, the letter then goes on to say that this Sirhan may not succeed in his attempt because he might be killed by a separate, hidden gunman, whom the letter describes in precise detail."

Charlotte shifted uneasily, sensing that this was no ordinary letter. Steven never discussed these kinds of things with her.

"The letter further states that the man who might kill Sirhan might also attempt to assassinate Richard Nixon. Now, normally, I don't spend much time or energy on these kinds of idle threats. I shoot them off to the FBI, CIA or Secret Service, but this one is different for a variety of reasons. First, there is a clear, detailed description of this Sirhan, as well as the man who is supposed to kill him, in order to stop RFK's assassination. And what is quite extraordinary is how the letter states the exact time and location Sirhan will attempt to kill Kennedy. According to the communique, Robert Kennedy will be mortally wounded on June 5th, shortly after midnight, Pacific Daylight Time, at the Ambassador Hotel in Los Angeles. I'll read the details from the letter. Steven reached into his shirt pocket for a pair of black-rimmed glasses and slipped them on.

> "Kennedy will start down a passageway
> narrowed by an ice machine against the
> right wall and a steam table to the
> left. Kennedy will turn to his left and
> shake hands with busboy Juan Romero—just
> as Sirhan Sirhan will step down from a

low tray stacker beside the ice machine, rush past the hotel ma tre d'h tel named Karl Uecker, and repeatedly fire an eight shot .22 LR caliber Iver Johnson Cadet 55 A revolver. The gunfire will wound five bystanders, including a 17 year old campaign aide named Irwin Stoll and labor organizer and Kennedy sup porter, Paul Schrade. All but Kennedy will survive."

Charlotte stared incredulous. "I don't understand. How could anyone know these things? I mean, how could it be that specific: wounding five bystanders; a named busboy shaking Mr. Kennedy's hand when he's shot? The writer is surely just making the whole thing up."

Steven lifted his eyes. "An agent called the Ambassador Hotel in L.A. and confirmed that Juan Romero is a 17-year-old busboy, and he is scheduled to work tomorrow night. There is a campaign aide named Irwin Stoll, and we know who Paul Schrade is, don't we? Needless to say, I contacted the FBI and the LAPD, and they are looking for Sirhan, and his possible killer, but I haven't received any updates yet. I have also learned that AID, or the Agency for International Development, is also involved. They are a front organization that provides cover for the CIA. I don't like their involvement, and I don't like the people they hang out with, namely, members of the mob they have worked with since the Bay of Pigs."

Charlotte stood up and raked a hand through her hair. "It just seems like it could be an elaborate fiction."

"There's more, Charlotte. Kent Reed mentioned something rather disquieting. He is aware that there are certain ongoing secret government experiments using clairvoyant talent and the use of telesthesia. Through intelligence, we have learned that the KGB is doing the same."

Charlotte's interest sharpened. "What is telesthesia?"

"In early occult and spiritualist literature, telesthesia was known as traveling clairvoyance, that is the ability to see remote or hidden objects clairvoyantly with the inner eye, or during alleged out-of-body travel."

Steven's face twisted into distaste. "I don't subscribe to this kind of thing, but Kent has connections with the subcultures of government and he is looking into it. What if we are dealing with the KGB? We have to consider all possibilities. I'd love nothing more than to have ignored this damn letter, but we don't have that luxury. Not after JFK's, Malcolm X's and Martin Luther King's assassinations."

Charlotte stared blankly at Steven, aware that he was locked in a struggling concentration.

Charlotte asked, "I'm sorry, when did you say Sirhan is supposed to attempt RFK's assassination?"

"Tomorrow night, after midnight, so early June 5th, assuming, of course, that the FBI or the LAPD doesn't find Sirhan, or that the unnamed assassin doesn't kill him first. If RFK does not die tomorrow night, then I suppose we may consider the letter to be a hoax. On the other hand, we must still be alert to the possibility of an assassination attempt on Richard Nixon. The letter stated quite dramatically that the potential assassin is a military man, very smart and professional."

Charlotte corralled her thoughts. "But doesn't it seem that if the letter is accurate, then it is a warning to stop both the assassin from killing Sirhan Sirhan, and Sirhan from killing Bobby Kennedy?"

They sat in a bewildering, chilly silence.

As Charlotte eased back down into her chair, Steven got up, keeping his steady eyes on the letter. "But what is even more disturbing, Charlotte, is that at the bottom of the letter, your own personal secret access code is clearly written, as well as a top-secret project that I assume you are not even aware of. Do you know of a top-secret project called ARRAY?"

Charlotte shook her head, feeling nauseous. "No…"

Steven sighed. "It does lend a very troubling credibility to all the information in the letter, doesn't it? Which is another reason we took all this business seriously."

Steven clamped his suspicious eyes on her. Charlotte squirmed in her chair, her mind stung by the information and allegation.

"I don't like this security breach, Charlotte. Is there anything about the letter you can tell me? Do you have any idea who might have written it? Can you tell me how someone, from the inside or the outside, got access to your security code?"

Charlotte could only stammer out, "Of… of course not. No… I mean I don't know, Steven."

"Well, I don't think we're dealing with a hippie sidewalk tarot card reader, are we? And it seems obvious that the writer of that letter is pointing a finger directly at you, so to speak."

A dark and fierce thought slid into Charlotte's mind. Was the entire situation somehow connected to that old lady?

Steven removed his glasses. "I'm sure you are aware that there will have to be an internal investigation into this, Charlotte."

Steven stared, Charlotte stared, and an icy silence grew between them.

CHAPTER 27

"I WAS THINKING, maybe we should take a couple days off, go down to the Maryland shore for a few days. Maybe even stay through the weekend," Charlotte said the next morning, Tuesday June 4th.

Paul glanced up from his scrambled eggs, his eyes surprised and probing. "What? What did you just say?"

He stuck a finger into his ear and wiggled it as if he wasn't sure he was hearing properly. "I'm sorry, did you say take a couple of days off and spend a weekend together?"

"Very funny," Charlotte said, flatly, as she blew on her black coffee and watched it ripple.

The family were gathered around the formica-topped kitchen table, having a rare weekday breakfast together. Charlotte was usually out of the house by 7 a.m.

Bright sun streamed in from open windows, and

yellow curtains billowed in a gentle breeze that carried the scent of honeysuckle and fresh cut grass.

Lacey stirred her bowl of *Fruit Loops*, staring hypnotically into them, whispering as if casting a spell, while Lyn ignored her eggs and distractedly played with her blonde curls.

"Please eat your eggs, Lyn," Paul said. "You said you wanted eggs this morning."

"I don't like eggs," Lyn said.

"Then why did you ask Daddy to make them for you?" Charlotte asked.

She shrugged. "I don't know."

"Do you want something else?" Paul asked.

Lyn brightened. "Pancakes!"

Lacey snapped out of her daydream, slapped her hands together and flashed a smile. "Yeah, pancakes," she exclaimed in rare agreement with her sister.

"We had pancakes yesterday," Paul said. "We can't have pancakes every day."

Lacey pouted and went back to stirring her imagined cauldron of some witch's brew and Lyn made a face.

"Why can't we have pancakes every day? Pancakes are good," Lyn said. "I don't like these eggs."

"If you eat your eggs this morning, we'll have pancakes tomorrow," Paul said. "We'll call it pancake Wednesday."

Lyn knew she was being manipulated, but she knew her father was truthful. "Okay..."

She pushed her eggs around while Lacey picked up one single fruit loop to examine it. Charlotte stared at her handsome husband, recalling with new pleasure their lovemaking the night before. She'd arrived home late, showered and slipped naked into bed next to Paul, who was sound asleep. She'd gently awakened him with warm, wet kisses and mischievous fingers. Soon, she was on top of him and he'd responded with strength and passion.

Afterwards, as they lay side by side, he whispered, "What happened?"

"What do you mean?" Charlotte asked, knowing perfectly well what he meant.

"When was the last time you've awakened and ravished me? Not that I'm complaining."

Her meeting with Steven had shaken and scared her, made her feel vulnerable. The last few days had been unsettling, to say the least, beginning with the bizarre conversation with that old woman. Charlotte knew something was out of sync, out of focus or just plain wrong. Did that old lady have something to do with the letter sent to the NSA? How could she? But how could it just be a coincidence?

"Are you asleep?" Paul asked, turning his body toward her, lifting up on an elbow. "Or have you tuned me out, tuning into some secret code at the NSA?"

"Sorry, no. I guess I'm just... I don't know, happy to be home with you and the girls."

She rolled to face him, seeing him in silhouette, and brushed his warm cheek with two fingers. "You do know that I love you very much, don't you? Almost from the first time I saw your slender body and that cowboy shirt with pearl buttons. I liked those pointy cowboy boots too."

"Well, I am from Austin, Texas, ma'am," he joked, in a thick southern drawl.

She laughed a little, enjoying the intimacy. "I loved those careful eyes and that dimple in your chin, like Cary Grant's."

Paul's voice was soft and tender. "I've always known you love me, Charlotte. I also know that when you leave me and the girls from time-to-time, both literally and emotionally, you'll eventually return to us. Welcome back again, Charlotte."

And then he held her in the soft curve of his arm, and they fell asleep.

Across the breakfast table, Charlotte gazed at Paul, as if she were trying to solve a problem. He noticed.

"Is everything all right?"

She allowed her eyes to explore his rugged face, the classic lantern jaw and the often amused, twinkling eyes. He had always been there for her, right from their first date, only a month after her mother had committed suicide. Charlotte had cried for days, blaming her cool, reserved and emotionally absent father.

With tears swimming in her eyes, she'd confessed to Paul, "My family had more issues than a magazine stand. My parents should have divorced."

Paul was a good listener, a good friend, and then a sweet and generous lover. He'd consoled her and been patient with her and loved her for who she was.

"Don't worry, Charlotte, you'll eventually find a way

to forgive your father. He's suffering too, you know. We all have certain capacities to love, some less, some more."

Charlotte wondered if she was more like her father than her mother. Was she cool and reserved and often emotionally absent?

Returning to the present moment, Charlotte nodded, in a half-smile. "Yes, I'm all right. I'm good, in fact. So, what do you say we blow off today and tomorrow and go to Ocean City or Virginia Beach, or New York… or anyplace?"

"I wish I could, but I've got that Nestlé ad campaign due by Monday. I'm going to have to work most of the weekend to finish it."

Charlotte sipped her coffee, staring down. "It was just an idea."

"What about next weekend?" Paul asked.

Her eyes shifted uneasily. "Yeah, maybe."

CHAPTER 28

Charlotte felt like a caged lion. She worked for a time, then paced, then smoked, then drank another cup of coffee—she'd lost track of how many cups she'd consumed—performing every task with nervous distraction. Her agitated thoughts wouldn't settle or focus.

In a meeting with a colleague, she was impatient and irritable, communicating in a brusque, hurried way. Time seemed to stop. She glanced at her watch incessantly, as well as at every clock she passed in the hallways and in the conference room.

She called Paul three times. He was in meetings. She called Florence to check on Lacey and Lyn. The girls were down the street at a friend's house. Had Florence already told her that? Yes. Her mind was a tangle of dread and fear.

It was Tuesday, June 4th.

Charlotte sat at her desk, staring disconsolate.

Where was the old woman at that moment? If there was an assassin, where was he?

By late afternoon, Charlotte stood at her window, gazing out at a ragged tear of light piercing through dark purple and heavy gray clouds, and she watched an airplane arrowing skyward until it disappeared.

She had to go home. Having dinner with Paul, Lyn and Lacey would help to distract her and steady her frayed nerves. There would be no conversations about the old lady or the letter to the NSA or anything having to do with her work. Promptly, at 5:30 p.m., Charlotte left the office and drove home.

△△△

Charlotte awakened abruptly. She glanced at the clock on the night table. It was 2:34 a.m. She gently left the bed, grabbed a robe and belted it as she started down the stairs, putting a fist to a yawn.

As she paced the living room, the themes from the day before kept crowding in on her. Should she have forced Paul to take her and the girls on a trip? Was it possible something horrible was going to happen to them? Was that old lady the writer of the letter to the NSA? Was she involved in some sort of KGB clairvoyance project? If so, why did she warn *her* that something was going to happen? Was she feeling guilty about being a Russian spy?

She was startled when she heard Paul's footsteps. "Charlotte, what's going on? Why are you up? It's late, or early," he said, with a wide, cavernous yawn.

Should she tell him? But where would she begin?

"Nothing really. I have a little indigestion, that's all. I guess I'm not used to being home for supper and eating Florence's fried chicken. I ate too much."

Paul approached her and rubbed her back. "I got your messages today. I called you back. Did you get my message?"

"Yes."

"Your voice sounds tense. Anything you want to talk about?"

"No… It's just work."

"Is there anything you can tell me?"

Charlotte put her face in her hands and shook her head.

"That means you'll be working late again tonight, right?"

Charlotte's voice began small and apologetic. "Well… There is something pretty serious going on."

"Isn't there always? Not that I'm criticizing your dedication to your job."

"Yes, you are, and maybe you should."

"You just don't sound like yourself, and you called me three times today and you were home at 6:30 and you avoided talking to me after the girls were in bed. Are you sure you're all right?"

Charlotte lowered herself in her chair. "I just wish we'd gone away."

"If it means that much to you, then let's do it. In the morning, I'll tell boss Charlie that I have to leave town on family business, and I'll take my work with me."

Charlotte sighed, and it made a whooshing sound.

"It might be too late."

"What do you mean, too late? Charlotte, what is going on?"

A curtain of rain slid across the windows. Startled, Charlotte pivoted toward it.

"I didn't know it was supposed to rain," she said.

Paul knew by now when it was futile to ask questions. He walked to the liquor cabinet, took down a half bottle of brandy, found two snifters, and poured them each a couple of ounces. He brought her a glass and they toasted, the snifters chiming.

"Here's to rainy nights and a pretty wife," he said.

She smiled. "Such a romantic."

Paul took a sip. "Why not? Maybe we should start a fire and make love."

"And what if the girls wake up and find us?"

He shrugged. "Then they'll learn about the birds, the bees and the Vances, romping in the living room."

But Charlotte remained remote. They sat on the couch and listened to the rain in silence. Charlotte sipped her drink slowly, pensively. Paul knew that when she was in a mood, she was not interested in the birds and the bees. He took the rest of the brandy in one go, got up and returned to the cabinet, pouring himself another. He tossed it back like a shot and set the glass down.

"Come back to bed, honey. I'll smother you with kisses and sing you Beatles' songs." The booze had loosened his mood and he began to sing, very off key, as he took her hands and tried to lift her from the couch. "*He loves you, yeah, yeah, yeah… with a love like that, you know you should be bad..."*

Charlotte laughed. "It's not 'bad,' it's 'glad'. And for heaven's sake, stop singing. You have many talents, Paul, but one of them is definitely not singing."

She remained seated.

Paul dropped her hands. "Okay, well I'm going back to bed. I'll sleep like a baby now." He stooped and kissed her. "Good night, darling," he said softly, then ambled down the hallway and up the stairs.

At 3:35 a.m., Charlotte was taking the snifters to the kitchen when the phone rang. Within seconds, she'd snatched the green wall phone receiver. "Hello?"

"Charlotte, it's Steven Case." He sighed. "Robert Kennedy's been shot."

The blood seemed to drain to her feet. "Did it..." she stopped, unable to release the words, not wanting to release the words.

"Yes, Charlotte. It all happened exactly the way the letter stated it would happen."

Charlotte felt her knees grow rubbery. Her mind seemed to go into spasm.

"Will Bobby live?"

Steven shook his head. "Doubtful. He has a bullet in the brain. He's at Good Samaritan Hospital."

Charlotte dropped into a kitchen chair, trembling. "Is there any word about the other guy? The man who was supposed to kill Sirhan?"

Charlotte could picture Steven inhaling a breath, all numb composure, ever the professional. "The LAPD spotted a man fitting his description, strolling just north of Hollywood and Vine, near the Capital Records building. As they approached him, he pulled a gun and fired. He struck two officers before a third fired back. He's dead. He had no ID."

Charlotte worked hard to break through the fog of despair and disbelief.

Steven continued. "I can only speculate as to why neither the CIA nor the LAPD were able to find and stop Sirhan Sirhan. And then there's a report about the possibility of a girl in a polka-dot dress being involved. It's all a confused mess right now."

Charlotte rose to her feet, reached for a tissue and dabbed at her wet eyes.

"Come into the office as soon as you can, Charlotte," Steven said. "And be prepared to put in some long hours for the next few days."

Without hesitation, Charlotte climbed the stairs, quietly pulled some clothes from her closet and dressed in the bathroom. She was backing out of her driveway within fifteen minutes. She had left Paul, Lyn and Lacey all sound asleep.

CHAPTER 29

Barely awake and yawning, Jay Anderson was behind the wheel of his Chevy Belair, and 76-year-old Charlotte sat stiffly in the passenger seat. It was 3:55 a.m., and they were traveling toward Marlow Heights. Charlotte looked anxiously at her watch. If nothing had changed due to her time travel, the fire would start at about 4:30 a.m.

Earlier, a light rain had fallen, washing the streets. With her window rolled down, Charlotte inhaled the sweet scent of rain and spring flowers. She gazed up and saw a crescent moon swimming through broken, dark clouds.

There was a certain release in being in motion, and Charlotte felt a surge of energy now that she was finally on the last leg of her time travel journey.

Several times, Jay had tried to ask questions or initiate conversation, but each time, Charlotte had given only clipped answers, or had remained altogether silent. After he'd arrived at the Willard Hotel lobby an hour before and they were in the car, she had given him a sealed 9x12 envelope containing the letter she had written to young Charlotte, along with her account of all the events which had led up to that night. Inside was also the family photo she'd brought from 2018, as well as the safe deposit box number, the password and the key. She had placed $40,000 in cash in the safe deposit box for Young Charlotte. Jay had looked at the envelope, confused.

"I want you to do something for me," Charlotte had said.

"Anything, you know that."

"Give this to the person it's addressed to if anything happens to me."

Jay had drawn back, twisting up his lip in protest. "What is this all about? Nothing is going to happen to you."

"Please, Jay. It is very important. Please promise me you'll deliver it in a week if anything happens to me. I know I can trust you."

His eyes shifted about. "You're scaring me a little, you know."

"Please, Jay."

He shrugged a shoulder. "Okay, if that's what you want."

Charlotte had then reached into her purse and drawn out a letter-sized envelope. "This is the money I owe you."

Jay's face pinched up. "What are you talking about?"

"We had a deal. I agreed to pay you if you were my chauffeur. That was our deal."

"I don't want your money. Don't insult me. We've come a long way since last Thursday. Put your money away."

Charlotte had held his eyes, softly. "Your wife Sally Ann was a very lucky woman, Jay. You're a very special man."

"Aw, stop it, I've got plenty of faults. Just wait until you get to know me better."

She touched his arm. "Thank you for everything."

"You sound like this is the end or something. I don't know why we're going on this drive so early in the morning, but the fact that I'm taking you, without questions, should prove that I want to be with you, no matter what."

They drove to Temple Hill Road and turned right on Leslie Avenue. It was time to implement the first part of her plan. As instructed, Jay stopped near a lighted public phone booth. Charlotte left the car, walked to the booth and entered.

With her lips pulled tightly together, she inserted a dime, dialed her former home number and let it ring. When she heard Paul's sleepy voice say "Hello," she spoke quickly.

"Paul, this is a friend. Please do as I say and don't ask questions. The house is about to catch on fire. Take the girls now and leave the house."

As expected, Paul was drowsy and irritated. "Who is this?"

"Please just do as I say. It is a matter of life and death."

Paul hung up.

Undaunted, Charlotte returned to the car, slipped in and closed the door.

"What now?" Jay asked.

They sat in a cocoon of silence before Charlotte turned to him. "I have one more thing I'd like you to do for me, Jay."

"Are you going to tell me what's going on?"

"When it's all over, I'll tell you everything. I promise."

Charlotte glanced down at her watch. "I'm going to get out and walk the rest of the way to the house. I want you to wait here, and then at exactly 4:20, I want you to call the fire department and report a fire at 2407."

She handed him a sheet of paper with the house address on it. Jay squinted a look at it and then slowly, his suspicious eyes came to hers.

"I know where the house is. We've been there twice. Calling the fire department on a false alarm is a crime… a very serious crime."

"It won't be false."

Jay's expression expanded in sudden anxiety. "What are you going to do, Charlotte?"

She took his hand and patted it, managing a nervous smile. "Don't worry. I'm going to do something I should have done fifty years ago. Please, Jay, make that call. Will you promise me?"

"Are you still working for the government, Charlotte? Is that what this is about?"

"I don't have time to explain right now. Please, will you make the call?"

He sighed heavily and faced away. "All right... But this is the last thing I'll do without an explanation."

Charlotte leaned and kissed him on the cheek. "You're a good man, Jay. Thank you."

She exited the car, leaving Jay shaking his head.

Charlotte started forward, making noiseless footsteps, as a humid breeze swept in. She passed nice homes and well-kept lawns, and she had to cross the street to avoid harassing a barking dog that stood on hind legs against a backyard fence.

Her strategy was simple: According to the old fire inspector report, the fire began somewhere between 4:30 a.m. and 4:45. At 4:25, she was going to stride up the walkway of the house, climb the stairs and wait on the porch until 4:30. She'd start ringing the doorbell and pounding on the door until she saw lights come on. She would keep pounding until Paul came to the door.

The day before, she had scouted out the house. She'd asked Jay to take her there before they drove to his place for TV dinners and a movie. She wanted to see Paul return home from work, wanted to witness Lacey and Lyn boil out of the house to meet him and be gathered up in his arms. The impact of seeing them again had taken her breath away. Her heart ached, her emotions nearly overwhelming her.

Irrationally, she'd wanted to burst from Jay's car and run to them, hold and kiss them, and tell them everything was going to be okay.

Charlotte pressed on, now only about a block away from the house. She saw a flash of lightning in the distance and turned her head away as a car approached, its head lights glaring.

Her pulse raced, and she heard the thud of her heart in her ears. She was almost there. Finally, after a lifetime of regret, she could right all the wrongs.

Her once sure stride began to wobble. Her color went sick. A hammer blow struck her heart and she cried out in pain. As the world veered and tipped and spun away, Charlotte clawed at her chest. A heavy wind pushed at her. She staggered, as pain surged and squeezed her heart like a vice grip.

She stumbled toward a nearby lawn as she began to lose focus. When she opened her mouth to call out for help, she only managed a feeble, hollow wheeze. She knew it was the hopeless and terrible sound of a dying woman. Even then she fought to stay on her feet, reeling about like a drunken woman.

She crumbled like a rag doll onto the damp grass, arms reaching out toward her house. In her head she screamed and called for help. Just a little further. Please, God, just a few more steps and she would save her family. **The wind gasped and circled.**

She managed to gulp in an agony of breath and let it out harshly. A slashing pain knifed through her body and still she clawed at the ground, eyes wide, mouth open, silently screaming for help.

As the light drained from her eyes, the first wisps of smoke were rising from the house at 2407.

CHAPTER 30

On the Baltimore-Washington Parkway, 26-year-old Charlotte drove like a madwoman, weaving in and out of lanes, laying on her horn whenever she encountered slow drivers. She was listening to the radio broadcasts about the assassination of RFK. She was almost at the office when the image of the old woman's piercing eyes rose before her, confronting her. Charlotte grew short of breath, as panic filled her like a cold liquid. If the letter was true—if everything had happened as the writer had said it would, and if the writer was the old woman, then what about the woman's warning to her?

```
"Whatever you do, take your family and
leave town by June 4th.  Please listen
to me and do this, Mrs. Vance."
```

Charlotte took the next exit, changed direction and sped off toward home. The car bounced and ramped, bending around curves, tires squealing, Charlotte's hard, determined eyes locked on the road. As she whipped the car onto Leslie Avenue, her heart jumped, and she made a sound of terror. As she approached her house, she saw an orange flickering light in the upstairs window, and billowing smoke rising from the roof.

She skidded to the curb, cut the engine and bolted from the car, leaving the car door open. As she sprinted up the walkway, she heaved in hot dry breath, mounting the stairs. Fumbling in her purse for her keys, she finally inserted a key into the lock, turned it and put a shoulder to the door. Inside, she coughed, acrid billowing smoke attacking her throat and lungs. She knew the house was about to be engulfed in flames.

Charlotte was only vaguely aware of distant wobbling sirens, piercing the night, as a hook-and-ladder truck was racing to the scene.

In a dead run, Charlotte charged up the stairs, an arm covering her mouth, as a wall of shimmering heat engulfed her. With the flat of her hand she hit the partially opened bedroom door. Through thick, rolling smoke, she saw Paul on the bed, not moving. Fire licked at the curtains, their bathroom already an inferno. Undaunted, she scrambled over to him, and through burning slitted eyes and a hacking cough, she reached him, tugging, screaming and slapping his face. Finally, he stirred, coughing violently.

"Get up," she yelled. "Get up!"

She pulled and yanked until Paul pushed up while

Charlotte threw off the sheet. Dressed only in his bottom pajamas, Paul clumsily swung his bare feet to the hot floor.

"Come on, we have to get the girls!" Charlotte yelled.

That galvanized him, and using Charlotte's shoulder for support, they stumbled out of the bedroom and across the hall where the girls slept.

Bursting inside a now burning room billowing with ugly, curling smoke, the parents staggered to the bedsides. Both girls were listless and unconscious.

Paul grabbed Lacey, lifting her into his protective arms. Charlotte seized Lyn, clutching her tightly against her shoulder. She and Paul ducked away and had just meandered away from the fire when it exploded a window and burst through the room.

Punished by the smoke and blinding heat, Charlotte and Paul blundered down the stairs, drenched in sweat, and in a last gasp of effort, managed to escape the house just as the hook-and-ladder truck arrived. Firemen sprang into action, shouting commands, tugging at hoses, and encircling the house. Soon, water surged from the hoses, arching up, attacking the spreading fire that lit up the night.

On the front lawn, Charlotte called for help and two firemen hurried over with oxygen. Paul handed Lacey over and then he collapsed into a spasm of coughing.

Minutes later the firemen clapped an oxygen mask over Lacey's and Lyn's noses and mouths.

One fireman glanced up to see Charlotte's terrified face. He said, "Don't worry. They'll be fine. You got them out in time."

When an ambulance arrived, Paul and Charlotte were swiftly treated for minor burns and smoke inhalation. As they lay on stretchers, they watched in horror as the roof buckled and plunged, and the walls collapsed into great sweeping plumes of fire.

And then Charlotte lay back and shut her eyes. She whispered a silent prayer of thanks to the old woman who had saved their lives.

△△△

Seventy-six-year-old Charlotte Wilson was taken to George Washington University Hospital and was pronounced dead at 6:30 a.m. on June 5, 1968.

Jay Anderson had found her sprawled on the lawn, and he was by her side, holding her hand when the ambulance arrived. As it drove away, he stood in the lonely, helpless night, aware of the burning house just down the block, but he didn't move toward it. A concerned neighbor, wearing a housecoat and slippers, asked if he was all right, but Jay didn't hear the man. He just stood staring, sad and lost.

Two days later, as he was searching his glove compartment looking for a flashlight, he found a bulging manila envelope with his name written on it. He sat back and opened it. To his astonishment, it was filled with 100-dollar bills that totaled eleven thousand dollars. The hand-written note said:

Dear Jay:
You were an expert and courteous chauf

feur; a dear friend and I dare say you would have been a wonderful husband. Please ac cept this little token of my gratitude for all you have done for me. Believe that it comes from a weak, but a full heart.

*With love,
Charlotte*

EPILOGUE
2018

Cyrano Conklin was in his office, bouncing a tennis ball on the wood floor. Then he threw it against the wall, caught it, threw it again —a slow and mechanical game that went on for over five minutes.

When his phone rang, he aimed the ball at his wastebasket and, in a little jump shot, released the ball. It hit the rim, glanced off and bounced to the other side of the room. He shook his head in weary disappointment and reached for the phone.

"Mr. Conklin, there's a woman here to see you. She said she has an appointment."

"What is her name?"

"Charlotte Vance."

He paused, screwing up his lips in thought. "An appointment?"

"Yes, sir... just a minute. She's telling me something." The secretary cleared her voice.

"Yes, well, Mrs. Vance says that it's a 50-year appointment."

Cyrano lowered himself down into the leather swivel chair and swiveled back and forth, his mind alive with circumspection. "Well, I suppose you'd better send her in. Oh, and escort her into the conference room, if you would please."

Cyrano was suddenly distracted by two flowerpots lingering on the windowsill. He made a sour face. He didn't know what the flowers were. His wife had brought them months ago, mumbling something about the office needing a woman's touch. He frowned at the flowers, feeling a pang of guilt. The poor, wilting things looked at him as if they were being held prisoner, withering away in their chipped clay flowerpots. Did they receive too much light? Not enough light? Did they need water? Had he watered them this week? Who could remember such things? The whole flower thing perplexed him.

He grabbed his paper cup half filled with water and drizzled them, nodding, proudly, as if he'd just saved a life.

Minutes later, Cyrano entered the well-appointed conference room and was surprised to see a tall, vital woman, with clear eyes, a radiant face and short, silver gray hair. He guessed her age at seventy-five, maybe seventy-six, but she possessed a fine carriage and a confident demeanor.

She stood, and he offered her his hand.

"Mrs. Vance, I presume?" Cyrano asked, pleasantly.

"Charlotte Vance, yes. Please call me Charlotte."

She looked at him rather strangely, he thought. He noticed an old manila envelope on the table.

"Well, I hope you're feeling well on this hot August morning. Please, sit down, Charlotte."

Cyrano sat opposite her, folded his hands, and inhaled and then released a breath, signaling it was time to begin.

"Now, what can I do for you?"

Charlotte lifted and settled her shoulders. "I thought you might know me. I thought you might be expecting me. You don't seem to."

He sat stiffly, with a tolerant smile. "I'm afraid I don't know you, Mrs. Vance… Charlotte. To my receptionist, you mentioned a 50-year-old appointment?"

Charlotte's eyes rested on the manila envelope. "I don't quite know where to begin. I'm sure I'm at the right place. This is TEMPUS, isn't it?"

Cyrano nodded. "Yes."

"And, obviously, you are Cyrano Conklin."

"I am one and the same."

Charlotte blinked around the room and gave a little shake of her head, as if perplexed.

"Then I don't know why I'm here."

Cyrano leaned forward, his expression turning curious. "Perhaps you can just tell me why you came? Did someone send you?"

Charlotte looked at him pointedly. "Yes, someone did."

"And who would that be?"

Charlotte reached for the manila envelope and then rested her hand on it. "Mr. Conklin... is TEMPUS involved with time travel?"

Cyrano studied her carefully. The skin around his eyes tightened. "Time travel?"

"Yes..."

Cyrano sat back. "Charlotte, TEMPUS is a research organization whose primary focus is on Suspended Animation, which literally means, putting life on hold. The preferred scientific term for the procedure is emergency preservation and resuscitation."

Charlotte stared hard while Cyrano continued.

"Not to bore you with details, it is a surgical technique that replaces all a patient's blood with a solution to cool the body down. This gives doctors the time to fix injuries without losing patients to blood loss. We here at TEMPUS are going one step further. We are doing the very real research that involves cryosleep. It is not too dissimilar from what you've probably seen in movies. We are experimenting with sedatives, IV drips, catheters, and a genuine cooling of the body to slow the body's metabolism down."

"And what will this be used for?" Charlotte asked.

"For space travel and, how should I say? For wealthy people who may want to live very long lives. They are our main donors."

Charlotte lowered her eyes. "I see. Obviously, TEMPUS has nothing to do with time travel then?"

"No, Charlotte. I'm afraid time travel is the stuff of science fiction and romance novels."

Charlotte slid the manila envelope across the table

to Cyrano. Their eyes met, his concerned, hers determined. "Would you please read the contents of that envelope and give me your impression? One account is from a woman named Charlotte Wilson. The other account is from me. I think you'll find them, if nothing else, at least fascinating."

Cyrano ran his hand across the envelope. "Who are you, Charlotte?"

"When you read that account, then you'll know. Shall I stay while you read? I promise, it will be worth your time."

Cyrano appeared doubtful.

"You are in that account," Charlotte said, waiting for his reaction.

His eyebrows lifted. "I… How could I?"

His voice trailed off as he took the envelope, opened it and tugged out the hand-written manuscript. He flipped through some pages, casually skimming them. When his eyes lifted, they held irritation. "Is this some kind of prank?"

Charlotte shook her head. "I don't know what it is. After you have finished reading it, perhaps you'll be able to tell me."

Charlotte rose to her feet. "Perhaps I should return this afternoon?"

Cyrano nodded. "If you wish…"

△△△

Charlotte returned at 3:30 that afternoon. Once again, the secretary escorted her to the conference room, where Cyrano and a woman were waiting. The woman introduced herself as Kim Stein. She was in her 40s and quite thin, with large startling dark eyes. Tattoos covered her entire left arm, and she exuded warmth and friendliness.

After they were all seated, Cyrano tapped the manila envelope with a finger and looked pensive.

"I hope you don't mind that I made a copy and allowed Kim to read your account as well."

"Not at all," Charlotte said.

Kim said, "According to the account, you met the woman who claimed to have time traveled, was an older version of you, and helped save your family from perishing in a fire?"

"Yes. As you have read, I met her, and as you can imagine, it was a rather startling and unforgettable experience."

Kim swung her gaze first to Cyrano and then back to Charlotte. "Charlotte, it is not our place to challenge or doubt you. We at TEMPUS can only say we have absolutely no knowledge of this."

"Then how do you explain it? How do you explain that both of you are mentioned at various times in the account? How do you explain that in June 1968, a man appeared at our apartment and handed me that envelope?"

Cyrano held Charlotte's eyes. "We can't explain it."

He spread his hands, then closed them. "It is an extraordinary story. Beyond that, I have no rational explanation. Perhaps the writer's intention was to write a novel, a very entertaining novel, but nothing more than that."

Charlotte sat quietly for a time, finally focusing her eyes on them. "When I was a young woman, I was all appetite and ambition. That woman in the account saved me, and she saved my family. I left the NSA in 1970, went back to school and became a psychologist, specializing in family counseling. I retired six years ago. It was a very rewarding career. My two daughters married and had children, and now I have five grandchildren and one great grandchild. My husband, Paul, is still in good health. We have been married almost fifty-five years. None of it would have happened if that woman… whoever she was… had not met me and warned me."

Charlotte paused, thoughtfully, before continuing. "If you were able to help her return to 1968, then I thank you, and please thank the entire team. By the way, is Alex Mason around?"

Charlotte shrewdly measured their reaction. There was none.

Cyrano said, "No, Charlotte. We don't know an Alex Mason. He has never worked with us in any capacity."

Charlotte arose. "Well, then. I'll be going. Thank you for your time."

Cyrano and Kim stood up. "Charlotte, would you mind if we kept this account? Just as a kind of reference, mind you?"

Charlotte flashed a hint of a smile. "No… keep it. I won't be needing it anymore. For me, it's all finished."

After she was gone, Kim and Cyrano sat in a loud

silence.

"Do you think she knew?" Kim asked.

Cyrano pursed his lips up in thought and tented his fingers. "The old Charlotte would have. I suspect Charlotte Two has her suspicions... but I do believe, as she said, it is all finished for her. The old NSA discipline in her will keep her quiet, and that was another reason we chose the old Charlotte to begin with, wasn't it? I firmly believe she will respect the integrity of this ongoing project."

"Too bad about Alex," Kim said, sadly. "You're sure the photos were accurate?"

"Yes, as I believe I mentioned just the other day, Dieter managed to find the CIA file from June 5th and the events surrounding Alex's death. The photos of his deceased body confirmed he was killed, but the details had been purged. I wonder what went wrong. Obviously, old Charlotte didn't know."

"I suppose we'll never know," Kim said.

Cyrano eased back, tapping the end of his nose with a finger. "Frankly, I was never very enthusiastic about his mission. I went along with it because, without him, we would have never gotten TEMPUS off the ground. Frankly, I never thought the whole piggyback thing would work. I'm surprised he made it to 1968."

Kim smiled. "Should we contact the rest of the team and break out a bottle of Champagne?"

Cyrano nodded. "Oh yes, more than one. After all, we have just learned that after years of wandering in the dark, and three failures, we have finally made time travel a reality."

"Have you decided what our next project will be?"

Cyrano stood and reached for the manila envelope. "We have several candidates to consider. I suggest we drink some Champagne and then get right to it."

As they were about to leave the room, Cyrano turned to Kim with an outstretched hand.

"By the way, well done."

△△△

Charlotte started her car, left the parking lot and entered the flow of traffic, heading toward Chevy Chase, Maryland. She glanced back into her rear-view mirror at the three-story red brick building she'd just left, with its dark green zig-zag fire escape. She lowered her sunglasses and began to laugh. Her laugh was small at first, just an intimate, personal laugh, but then it swelled and deepened, until it reached a zenith and then faded back into a reflective smile.

She took a detour to the Willard Hotel and parked across the street from it, and her mind drifted and remembered Jay Anderson. They'd met only once, when he'd handed her the manila envelope all those years ago. Their conversation had been polite and brief. There were many things she had wanted to ask, but he hadn't lingered.

When a text dinged in from Paul, asking where she was, she swung the car back into traffic and started home. Paul was anxiously waiting. They'd already started packing for their second honeymoon to Paris, but they had much left to do before their flight the next day.

In Paris, they would be just two old American tourists, relaxing in the sidewalk cafes, lingering in the museums and enjoying the rich food and wine. They would wander the streets together, sharing their love and all their golden memories.

And while in Paris, Charlotte would visit Sacré-Coeur Basilica in Montmartre and light a candle for her, for the woman who had saved her life and her family's lives. On her knees, Charlotte would whisper a prayer, thanking the woman for a full and rich life. For a beautiful life.

THANK YOU!

Thank you for taking the time to read *Time Sensitive*. If you enjoyed it, please consider telling your friends or posting a short review. Word of mouth is an author's best friend, and it is much appreciated.

Thank you,
Elyse Douglas

Other novels by Elyse Douglas that you might enjoy:

The Christmas Diary

The Summer Diary

The Other Side of Summer

The Christmas Women

The Christmas Eve Letter (A Time Travel Novel) Book 1

The Christmas Eve Daughter (A Time Travel Novel) Book 2

The Lost Mata Hari Ring (A Time Travel Novel)

The Christmas Town (A Time Travel Novel)

The Summer Letters

The Date Before Christmas

Christmas Ever After

Christmas for Juliet

The Christmas Bridge

Wanting Rita

www.elysedouglas.com

EDITORIAL REVIEWS

THE LOST MATA HARI RING – A Time Travel Novel
by Elyse Douglas

"This book is hard to put down! It is pitch-perfect and hits all the right notes. It is the best book I have read in a while!
5 Stars!"
--Bound4Escape Blog and Reviews

"The characters are well defined, and the scenes easily visualized. It is a poignant, bitter-sweet emotionally charged read."
5-Stars!
--Rockin' Book Reviews

"This book captivated me to the end!"
--StoryBook Reviews

"A captivating adventure…"
--Community Bookstop

"…Putting *The Lost Mata Hari Ring* down for any length of time proved to be impossible."
--Lisa's Writopia

"I found myself drawn into the story and holding my breath to see what would happen next..."

--Blog: A Room Without Books is Empty

Editorial Reviews

THE CHRISTMAS TOWN – A Time Travel Novel
by Elyse Douglas

"*The Christmas Town* is a beautifully written story. It draws you in from the first page, and fully engages you up until the very last. The story is funny, happy, and magical. The characters are all likable and very well-rounded. This is a great book to read during the holiday season, and a delightful read during any time of the year."

--Bauman Book Reviews

"I would love to see this book become another one of those beloved Christmas film traditions, to be treasured over the years! The characters are loveable; the settings vivid. Period details are believable. A delightful read at any time of year! Don't miss this novel!"

--A Night's Dream of Books

Editorial Reviews

THE SUMMER LETTERS – A Novel
by Elyse Douglas

"A perfect summer read!"
--Fiction Addiction

"In Elyse Douglas' novel *The Summer Letters*, the characters' emotions, their drives, passions and memories are all so expertly woven; we get a taste of what life was like for veterans, women, small town folk, and all those people we think have lived too long to remember (but they never really forget, do they?).
I couldn't stop reading, not for a moment. Such an amazing read. Flawless."
5 Stars!
--Anteria Writes Blog - To Dream, To Write, To Live

"A wonderful, beautiful love story that I absolutely enjoyed reading."
5 Stars!
--Books, Dreams, Life - Blog

"The Summer Letters is a fabulous choice for the beach or cottage this year, so you can live and breathe the same feelings and smells as the characters in this wonderful story."
--Reads & Reels Blog

ABOUT THE AUTHOR

Elyse Douglas

Elyse Douglas is the pen name for the married writing team Elyse Parmentier and Douglas Pennington. Elyse grew up near the sea, roaming the beaches, reading and writing stories and poetry, receiving a master's degree in English Literature. She has enjoyed careers as an English teacher, an actress, and a speech-language pathologist.

Douglas has worked as a graphic designer, a corporate manager, and an equities trader. He attended the Cincinnati College-Conservatory of Music and played the piano professionally for many years.

www.elysedouglas.com

BOOKS BY THIS AUTHOR

The Christmas Eve Series - Time Travel Romance - Five Books

In an antique shop, Eve finds an old lantern with a dusty letter hidden inside. It's dated 1885, and her name is written on it... And so, the series begins.

Time Change - Time Travel Romance

In 1948, a film star sees a strange man in her photos. In 2019, a writer sees a strange woman in his photos. Film star and writer occupy the same beach house—71 years apart.
In an extraordinary moment, they meet face-to-face.

Time Stranger - A Time Travel Novel

When a bomb strikes single mom Anne Billings and her young son in 1944 London, Anne is blown through time over half a century into the future. With the help of handsome Dr. Jon Miles, Anne desperately attempts to piece together her identity and return home.

Time Visitor - Time Travel Romance

A YOUNG WIDOW ENCOUNTERS a handsome, time-traveling Navy pilot from 1944, who force-lands near her home in 2005. They fall in love, but when an angry, powerful suitor discovers the Navy pilot's incredible identity, they must flee. They climb into the airplane and fly away... into another time.

Time Shutter

Equipped with a time travel camera, Caitlin Thompson escapes the grips of her dangerous half-sister by sending her to 1890. Seeking justice, Caitlin follows — but soon finds herself distracted by a handsome rogue, Jack Flint...

The Lost Mata Hari Ring - A Time Travel Novel

When Trace puts on a glittering ring and is vaulted back in time, she finds herself in the Paris of another era. Soon, she's swept off her feet by an irresistible British pilot, Edward... and the mysteries of a past life!

Time With Norma Jeane - A Time Slip Novel

A troubled young woman time slips into 1954 and

gets picked up on the side of a road by her idol, Marilyn Monroe...

The Christmas Diary Book One - A Novel

On a snowy night in a B&B, Alice Ferrell finds a lost diary written by a man fifteen years ago, and she sets off to find him...

The Christmas Diary Book Two - Lost And Found - A Novel

In their recently purchased B&B, Alice and Jack find an old diary in a lost-and-found bin in their basement, written in 1944.

Printed in Great Britain
by Amazon